STRANGE AND PERFECT ACCOUNT FROM THE PERMAFROST

Originally published in the Netherlands as
Waarachtige beschrijvingen uit de permafrost
by Koppernik in 2022.
COVER DESIGN Cooley Design Lab
LAYOUT Nikša Eršek
PUBLISHED BY Sandorf Passage
South Portland, Maine, United States
IMPRINT OF Sandorf
Severinska 30, Zagreb, Croatia
sandorfpassage.org
PRINTED BY Booksfactory.hr

2nd printing

Sandorf Passage books are available to the
trade through Independent Publishers Group:
ipgbook.com | (800) 888-4741.

Library of Congress Control Number: 2024950295

ISBN: 978-9-53351-533-5

Also available as an ebook;
ISBN: 978-9-53351-536-6

Nederlands
letterenfonds
dutch foundation
for literature

STRANGE AND PERFECT ACCOUNT FROM THE PERMAFROST

DONALD NIEDEKKER

Translated by Jonathan Reeder

SAN-DORF PAS-SAGE

SOUTH PORTLAND | MAINE

WHATEVER IT IS you seek, be it the spices of India, the morning, Ithaka, your father's love, any love at all, justice, dead souls, knighthood, a peer, someone to converse with, the comfort of a gypsy girl, the unicorn—go, my friend, I give you my voice, however you seek it, with a thousand wiles or with your pen, with a black ship, with painkillers on the nightstand, with a pistol on the nightstand, with a cardboard helmet, a horse, and a manservant, with a thermometer, with rolled-up pant legs, with shame and tears, growling behind barbed wire, by walking through the shade, pressing paper, collecting dew in April, moving your lips, go, my friend, do not lose heart, I give you my voice, with whomever you seek, with Gerrit de Veer, Jan Hillebrantsz, Jacob van Heemskerck, Lenaert Heyndricksz, and whoever else, with a varlet, with a pimple on your nose, even if you don't have a nose, with a bloodhound or with Rosinante, with a donkey or with thirty white-smocked Egyptian sailors, with the Three Marys, with a Jesuit and a humanist, with evil incarnate, with a tick from the left ear of a dog, go, my friend, go, I give you my voice, wherever you may be confined—in hell, in a Prussian valley, in, like me, the polar night, in a cellar, in a sanitarium on a Swiss mountain, in a summerhouse overgrown with grapevines and honeysuckle, in the maelstrom of your fancies, in your lost childhood that never was a childhood, in a Russian or Swedish summer, on a headland among seals, in a village hotel—go, go, my friend, I give you my voice, by any path you wish, around the North, through a forest of firs, straight up into the sky, over mountain passes, through a shady dale, over seven seas, following a caravan track, through swamps as you cling to slender birches, go, whoever you are, I give you my name, you are the eternal seeker, but whatever it is you seek, whatever, a ship's freightage, the dawning day, a faraway island, a passage, a beluga whale, riches, a peaceful old age, tea with jam on a saucer, van Gogh's ear, the sword Durendal, a kiss from Lancelot and Guinevere, Muhammad's toenail, I give you one name, the name Novaya Zemlya, Nova Zembla, New Land, New Earth, New World . . .

Go. Go, my friend.

Go.

THE CARTOGRAPHER REFLECTS. The clergyman reflects. The astronomer reflects.

On boundaries.

Boundaries of land and boundaries of the open sea. Boundaries God placed on man. Boundaries of the universe and boundaries on what we can know. Boundaries on measuring longitude. The Jacob's staff should be long obsolete by now. Boundaries beyond Cape Tabin.

Petrus Plancius is the cartographer. Petrus Plancius is the clergyman. Petrus Plancius is the astronomer.

He is, one could say, the triumvirate of the Northeast Passage. Whether I can compare this apostate of the Church of Rome with the Trinity, holy or not, is a matter that falls outside my very modest authority.

Petrus Plancius is familiar with the world of maps and with the stories pilots bring back with them. Observations, coastlines, depth measurements with a plumb line, anchor locations, prevailing winds, ocean currents, the behavior of birds, magnetic declination. He is familiar with the world of numbers and that of the Word.

When Petrus Plancius reflects, it is almost as though God himself is reflecting. Let us say, a cool, perhaps somewhat rigid, spirit, whereby every point is the midpoint of thoughts, theories, and doctrines.

Now, he reflects upon boundaries and stumbles upon a boundary in his memory. This irritates him. His memory is usually as readily accessible as the Bible. Infallible, a crystal clear, unerring edifice of references, allusions, and allegories that mirror themselves upon one another. Beyond the shadow of a doubt.

The coach, drawn by one gray and three fox-brown horses, bounced and lurched over a pitted dirt road. It passed fellow unfortunates also fleeing Brussels, Antwerp, and Bruges. Off on the shoulder, a father in a ragged felt coat doled out a flatbread and a sausage among three children who nestled up to him. No, Petrus Plancius could not look. The wheels clattered over a log bridge—was it the Rhine near Leiden?—and he had a flash of inspiration.

He should have written it down at once, but his quill pens, inkpot, and paper were in a chest lashed to the roof of the coach over which branches scraped.

Vexing.

And the noise of those branches.

All the more vexing is that now, with his sharpened pens ready for use, the paper unwritten and the inkpot uncorked, lying before him on the oak table under the model ship hanging from the beamed ceiling, a table large enough for a map of the world—sold to him by Cornelis Claesz on his second day in Amsterdam—he cannot for the life of him remember the inspiration. He had found the passage. But if you forget the premise, then that garbled catalog of theses, antitheses, and syntheses is of no use whatsoever.

Vexing.

He should not have looked out the coach window. At the woman in the generously pleated skirt of heavy cotton, who reached under her patched-up coat, unbuttoned a gray blouse, and nursed a baby, a tiny pink splotch in sackcloth, while a man trudged into the field. A few weeks ago, Plancius might have passed the woman on the market square in Brussels. Perhaps it was she who, with a wink and a saucy smile, had sold him the silk stockings. He had made a hasty exit.

A woman behind a tree lifted her skirt and, no, he couldn't bear to see it, not all those poor wretches, the resigned but determinedly advancing throng of exiles. There were cows too, windmills with their ceaselessly spinning sails, clouds, birds. A grass snake lay sunning itself on a warm stone on the bank of a brook. Yes, this was the Rhine delta at Leiden.

With a tug, he pulled the curtain shut.

He reflects.

He can reflect all he wants but will not be able to pilot that flash of inspiration into the harbor of his memory. It has gone adrift and shimmers on the horizon of his imagination. Every time Plancius thinks he can surprise it and reel it in with a clever association or image, it sidesteps him and darts out of sight, only, at the most inopportune moment—as he is climbing the steps to the pulpit for his sermon or attempting to persuade the Admiralty to approve a new expedition to the North—to resurface from the back of his thoughts like a curl of mist, a far-off scent, a vague melody, then waft past and, as soon as he focuses on it, promptly evaporate in the ethereal distance.

Vexing.

The renowned cartographer, the man behind explorations to the Northeast Passage, the unshakable theologist does not recognize the ability of one's memory to forget something but still remember that it's been forgotten. It would have made him less rigid, less dogmatic, less stubbornly convinced of the truth, less severe with those who think differently than he, those who do not share his faith, or, to put it another way—don't let him hear it—with those who are a tad more Catholic.

Nevertheless, he reflects.

Even when his wife, Johanna Geubels, enters his study, carrying a black lacquer tray with a steaming pot of nettle tea and a dish of dates, Wallachian nuts, and candied fruits. She sighs, which goes unnoticed, and sets it down on a corner of the table close to the map. Too close.

Vexing.

Let him reflect. It gives us the opportunity to take a closer look at the map. As she turns from the table to the door, Johanna Geubels tucks back a lock of ash-blonde hair that had come loose from under her linen cap.

The map.

NO, IT IS not the map Cornelis Claesz recently sold to Petrus Plancius. My memory is rusty and puts events side by side when, in fact, they were separated by at least a decade. Which stagecoach was Petrus Plancius in when he reflected on the Northeast Passage? Why hadn't he gone by ferryboat? My memory is not so much infallible, but of another order. More on that later.

On the drawing table under the model ship suspended from the ceiling is a representation of Northern Europe, captured in a network of parallels and meridians, and, at its heart, Novaya Zemlya. Creamy yellow and olive green color the map. A dotted line indicates the route of a ship. Lissome whales—apparently not the Greenland variety, which would be easy to recognize by their double blowholes and the V-shaped fans of spray—cavort in the sea surrounding the boomerang-shaped island. Seals poke their heads above the surface of the water.

The dotted line runs north of Norway toward a cluster of larger and smaller islands, "The New Land," which would later be known as Spitsbergen and, later yet, or perhaps earlier too, Svalbard. You can claim a land by naming it. There, too, the whales frolic and spray their fountains.

From this archipelago, the dotted line continues southward at first, and very soon splits into a northward and an eastward one, indicating at least two ships. The easterly line reaches the northernmost tip of Novaya Zemlya. The coast on the Kara Sea side has been left more or less unmarked, but the west coast's capes and bays are meticulously drawn and have Dutch names like Lange Nes, Swart Klip, Beerefort, Cruys Eylandt, Meelhaven, Het Leghen Landt. There is a Twisthoeck, a Beerhoeck, and a D'Eerste Hoeck, a Grote Bay, a Lomsbay, and a S. Lourens Bay.

With names, you can bend history to your will.

Around the northern cape with the Islands of Orange, just past Heemskerckse Hoek, is a wooden cabin with smoke coming out of its chimney. A cabin as a spouting whale. *Het Behouden Huys*, "The Sheltering House." Here, after IJshaven, the coastline simply stops. It is a blank patch that must still be filled in, a void awaiting new expeditions. It is knowledge that, despite the compass, the caliper, the latitude and longitude grid, cannot hide what it does not know.

WE SAW FOUNTAINS.

We saw gleefully spouting fountains above the sea.

In the fountains we saw mist.

Mist made of tiny droplets that lit up and then burst into a moment of rainbow.

And in that mist were droplets in which we saw yet more lit-up droplets, all of them identical and all of them sparkling and briefly winking with mother-of-pearl and then fleeting facets.

We saw dancing mist.

We saw a whale.

I CAN ZERO in on the cabin. By the haze of the lamps burning polar bear fat, sixteen men lie idly in their bunks, no more than partitioned wooden planks lining the rime-frosted walls. The chimney is a barrel that once held pickled herring, or flour, or salt pork. There is the ticking of a clock. This timepiece with its bell, chime hammers, and alarm had been intended as a gift for the Emperor of China.

We could also sail to Spitsbergen, which is not yet called this; its bluffs are a haven for birds, and its bays and fjords are a paradise for whales. A few years from now, it will be a place of human activity. They will flense whales and boil the blubber for oil.

Or we could have a look near the newly discovered Bear Island. A whale appears from below, first as an oval breaking the surface, growing steadily until it's the size of an island. Its maw opens. This is the port that opens only for you. Quite some few have preceded you, each through his own whale port. You need no password, no magic spell. You just have to take a step. One step. What are you waiting for? You go in a poltroon, you come out a prophet.

You could, if the stench doesn't knock you out, rest among a group of seals on a headland. Two swans alight, shed their plumage, and the Norns toss an egg back and forth. That is your fate.

Or sail into the waters of Arkhangelsk and report there to the governor, with the risk of being caught up in a carousel of dinners, balls, concerts, social calls, reciprocal social calls, and soirees that cannot be avoided without offending a knyaz or knyaginya.

If I now turn the spotlight back to the cabin, then I am lying in the middle of it, near the fire, wrapped in coarse wool blankets intended as merchandise.

I am the nameless crew member who died on January 27, 1597. Some claim it was January 26; a singleton who has completely lost count says the 28th. It was just past midnight on January 27 when I expired. My fellow travelers will have been as distressed—they were next, surely!—as they were relieved. I would no longer have to share in the meager rations of herring, groats, peas, and wine, and my fetid breath and excrement would no longer aggravate the air already made foul by fat, sweat, and smoke.

It was thus shortly after midnight, deep in the Arctic winter when it was night all day. A few days earlier, Gerrit de Veer and Jacob van Heemskerck had seen the sun peek briefly above the horizon. On January 24, under fine, clear skies with a westerly wind, they saw what they should not have seen, what they could not possibly have seen, but what they nonetheless saw. After my death too, the sun shone "in his full roundness," as they put it, just above the horizon. Willem Barentsz pursed his lips, paged, paged, paged, ahead, back, ahead in the volume

Ephemerides Josephi Scalae, ad annos duodecim, incipientes ab anno Domini 1589, better known as the *Almanac* by Giuseppe Scala, but nowhere in the tables for anno Domini 1597 showing the relative positions of the sun, moon, and planets could he find any confirmation of what had been observed.

Sometime later, Johannes Kepler would clarify what became known as the Novaya Zemlya effect as an arctic mirage. Prompted by measurements made by the Dane Tycho Brahe, he was able to formulate a law of refraction. Light from the unseen sun is trapped in the lower layers of the atmosphere; it can travel long distances around the curvature of the Earth and is reflected exactly where the horizon meets the atmosphere. And so, just like that, the sun was there a full two weeks before it should have been, and Willem Barentsz again combed through the table of the sun's positions. He was at least as obsessed by numbers, measurements, and accuracy as Petrus Plancius.

At the moment of celestial spectacle, polar mirage, hallucination, and delirium, I traded the temporal for the eternal. The eternal ice.

I am of small build. They did not need to dig me a large grave. Besides, they first had the snow to shovel through. In the German translation of *The True and Perfect Description of Three Voyages, So Strange and Wonderfull That the Like Hath Neuer Been Heard of Before*, likewise published in 1598 in Nuremberg in a translation by Levinus Hulsius, who had fled Ghent for that Southern German city, where he taught French and published books and would later move to the book city of Frankfurt—but ah, I'm rambling. In any case, the German edition of Gerrit de

Veer's travelogue includes a print depicting my funeral. Men armed with muskets shoot at polar bears. Arctic fox traps are set and cocked. Snowbanks pile up against the cabin. A group of men—one of them, the one holding the axe, I believe I recognize as Jacob Jansz Hooghwout—is skinning a polar bear. As they hack away at the snow, I lie there like a dead bumblebee with its forelegs folded together. Behind me, a polar bear is being buried. Whether the German illustrator meant anything by this, I can't say. Be that as it may, a female polar bear would later keep me company, winter after winter.

They prepared me a tidy grave. Jan van Buysen Reyniersz stood, musket at the ready, on the lookout for polar bears. The ground was frozen solid. I lay a bit cramped, with my broad, bony shoulders pressed against the ice walls. I got a glass of jenever splashed over my shroud. Willem Barentsz and Jacob van Heemskerck must have stashed it somewhere; we had no idea there was any. A waste of good jenever. I also could have done without the Bible reading and the psalms. It didn't occur to them to recite a poem, a line or two of Horace, not *exegi monumentum* per se, but *carpe diem* wouldn't have been so difficult, or if that escaped their memory and rules, then some stanzas from the Song of Songs. But what did they know of me?

Granted, I had been warned. But I insisted on wearing my leather hat with its broad, nonchalantly upturned brim, which went so well with my sharkskin gloves. After all, I was the balladeer, the bard, the rhapsodist. I refused to tug one of those ridiculous woolen caps over my head, with its smart blue, black, and white stripes, handy for a storm on deck perhaps, but otherwise too constricting, clamping one's skull so tightly that all that comes out are calculations, cargo contracts, clauses. Poetry? Not a chance.

I charged with a poet's panache out to the ice floes. And I caught my death of cold. I became the sick man who languished away. I let it happen. No odes to Cathay, China, or the Indies—we would never reach them anyway. As a poet you must know when your time has come.

So, on January 27, 1597, I snuffed it, and into the ground I went. That ground was a layer of snow and ice. A layer of snow that would never—the Little Ice Age was at its coldest—thaw. For four centuries I've been lying here frozen.

NOVAYA ZEMLYA IS everywhere.
Novaya Zemlya is everything.
Novaya Zemlya is my ruin.
Novaya Zemlya is my salvation.

WHAT ALL HAVE I collected in my ice grave? And what has my memory woven through it? What is there for me to tell? I traveled with shamans through both upper and nether worlds. Shock waves brought me news of earthquakes, tsunamis, crop failures, and volcanic eruptions, and they were joined by the whisper of underground voices, not all of which, admittedly, I was able to make out or decipher, but which did deposit a fertile layer within my memory.

Those layers piled up, and over time—a span of centuries—gravity did its work, and even in the forever-frozen ground, small volcanic outbursts occurred and higher-lying deposits broke through the older layers, allowing the sediments of memory to seep down to earlier times, mixing together the old with the new.

There's Novaya Zemlya, Petrus Plancius, the Northeast Passage, a clock, an astrolabium catholicum, walruses, and scurvy grass all jumbled up, and also amber, Grandmother's stories, an egg within an egg, Samoyeds, the Chinese Emperor and his daughter, a book merchant, Tycho Brahe, Johannes Kepler, Elling Carlsen, even Andrei Sakharov, a Finnish icebreaker, my cavalier hat, Mother at the spinet, a snow hare, and my Jewish tutor at the Latin school, whose black-speckled green eyes could just as easily fade into black eyes with a shimmer of malachite.

I must find a way to piece all this together into a more or less coherent narrative. But do cut me some slack. For four hundred years I have been lying in the frozen ground, more than four hundred years. Then you learn that there is no bigger deceit than consistency. Everything being interconnected—that kind of platitude. It's all about coincidence, sometimes dislodged for a second by the brief twinkle of causality.

I'll do my best to present the facts, episodes, half-overheard sentences, anecdotes, and all manner of trivia in as logical a context as possible—logical, that is, after the logic of a psyche frozen for centuries and only recently starting to thaw. My mind is a mishmash of senses being randomly inundated, without being subjected to any kind of order.

You must go easy on me.

But I will do my best.

I'll do my best.

IT WAS AN idea articulated in the maps, on the globes, in the journals and catchy-titled treatises that the curious and enterprising sixteenth century prided itself on. It spurred debates and adventures, it invited the wildest speculations; some poured all their energy, capital, and wherewithal into it, and although the underlying motive was monetary gain, the merchant's dream of throwing open the bountiful markets of the Orient, it was first and foremost an idea, just as truth is an idea, and summer and love and time and money are ideas. Illusions that, through common belief in them, become realistic and take on a life of their own so that the spurious premise vanishes out of view.

The Northeast Passage.

Like every idea, it exists in countless forms and variants, and its only basic rationale is the kaleidoscopic coalescing of its many facets. The Northeast Passage, the northerly route to Japan, China, and Cathay, whatever that country is, around the north.

Around the north . . .

As though the wind is yours to conjure up at will. They could just as well have tied their fortunes to the tail of an Arctic fox.

Where to begin?

With a map the second pilot takes from a tin cylinder? With the globe upon which the first pilot indicates a spot, traces a route? Or with the Admiralty, where a cartographer has gone to fetch the journals, logbooks, and coastal descriptions from the most recent maritime expedition to the North? Or where Petrus Plancius will submit the instructions for the upcoming journey?

You must forgive me a little *taedium vitae* after listening to crackling ice for four hundred years and a few decades. But it is the salt and pepper with which I spice my saturation. I have always needed pushback to take what came effortlessly to me—I only needed to shake the tree and its fruit fell into my lap—and deepen it with concentration.

Concentration is everything, said Damascius, my teacher at the Latin school. But what if one innately leans toward levity, play, diversion, dillydallying? My other teacher, Samuel Ben Yohai, saw that I needed a shake-up and sent me out into the world.

I can begin in the north, at what's come to be called the North Cape, at an English trading post on the Russian coast, a monastery on the White Sea. There, a single-sailed Russian lodya sets off, laden with skins and fish. As the wind and the sail do their work, the fishermen sing their sea shanty:

The wind is up, the deck's awash.
We're sailing full ahead.
The sun is rising with the tide,
And the Black Sea's turning red.

Or I'll begin where I already was. With a map. The map of Novaya Zemlya and its environs is still spread out on Petrus Plancius's desk in the serene candlelight. On the corner of the table is a teapot and a dish of nuts, dates, and brightly colored candied fruits—raspberry pink, lemon yellow, some green or another—bright for this study in brown tints, the ocher of leather volumes arranged systematically in the bookcases, Bibles (the Delft one too), works by Augustine, folios, song collections, the *Almagest* by Ptolemy, *Spieghel der Zeevaerdt* ("Mariner's Mirror") by Lucas Janszoon Waghenaer, mathematical treatises by Simon Stevin, *flameng françoys* dictionaries, Willem Barentsz's book of maps of the Mediterranean Sea, published by Plantijn in Antwerp, the bookseller Haller in Cracow, and the Calvinist printer Dolet of Lyon, already long ago, during the Inquisition, burned at the stake as a heretic. A galleon hangs from the rough-hewn ceiling beams above the desk. The room smells of parchment, wax, and nettles.

Plancius, whose name was Platevoet, feels the teapot with his fingertips. He shakes his head, mumbles to himself, and pours instead autumn-brown hazelnut liqueur from a carafe into a goblet of heavy green glass, on its stem four nubs, also of glass. The astronomer, geographer, cartographer, mathematician, preacher reflects on the boundaries of the world. On sea routes, the polar regions, open water, the conditions of ice along the coast, whether there is land covering the pole, vegetation at various latitudes.

He runs his hand over his beard, the palm feeling its full breadth. It is a recently acquired tic, perhaps one expressing satisfaction over a productive train of thought, or a habit of old age (he has aged prematurely), or something done absentmindedly (out of the question for Petrus Plancius).

Had he seen it well? It could not be true. It wasn't true. No, not true. No, no, no. But there, he saw it again. Just for an instant, too briefly to turn his gaze to that strange, bizarre impossibility. The image, however, remained stuck in his mind. A face that poked out of the hearth, upside down, grinning at him. There it is again: right under the hourglass on the mantel, a head sticking out of the stovepipe. Long, bony fingers pulling wide the corners of the mouth in a grotesque grimace.

No, no, he is overtired, he has sat for too long reading the Portuguese journals. They had cost him a pretty penny, procured via a clerk with connections in Lisbon; he'll charge them to the company. When he blows out the candle, he catches another glimpse of the goblin's head hanging upside down in the hearth.

Plancius leaves the glass of liqueur untouched on the table. The following morning it is empty.

MY FATHER TRADED in wood. He had acquired the rights to tracts in Poland—"My most profitable forests," he said. "Alas, without the right to hunt or fish, but oh, what timber!"—and Finland, which kept changing hands between the Swedes and the Russians; and the Finns, or whatever that folk there is called, all the more obsessively singing their magic songs. They possessed a musical instrument—a kind of lute, I believe—which could turn people into trees and stones, even into a lake.

Whenever he turned up again after a monthslong absence, wearing a sable coat, Father carried the scent of bears and deep woodlands. He also bore the weight of one who has traveled far. He brought bustle into the house, tumult, a flurry of activity, and with it the prospect of surprise.

Far different than the time spent with my mother: measured, honey-hued days immersed in affection and attention. She played the spinet, I did my sums and learned Latin and Greek words. Home had the serenity of an inland sea with small boats and rippling light.

Father dragged me into the world with his stories, his energetic gestures, his face ruddy from the outdoors. For every step he took over the cobbles along the quay, I needed three to keep up; he pointed out ferryboats, coastal vessels, a just off-loaded cargo of brazilwood, and hempseed from Riga. I saw him as the wind that billowed the sails, made windmill blades spin, and propelled his timber across the seas.

I respected my father, a naive, flimsy, child's respect that evaporated by the time I was thirteen. But my mother, I loved.

Father did card tricks and could make brightly colored scarves vanish and reappear at will. A clap of his hands, and a lizard walked across the table. He would hide a coin in his left hand, then close both fists alongside his body, and when he opened them again the coin appeared in his right palm. He would pluck a writing lead from my satchel and, with a wave, make it disappear, and a second later shake it out of one of his Polish house shoes with the curled-up toe.

Once he took a hard-boiled egg from his coat pocket. He held it out to me, but before I could take the egg, he drew it back and broke it open. Inside the egg was another egg, for it was an egg made of wood and the egg-in-the-egg was also wooden, light-brown lacquered wood with a few speckles so that it looked just like a real egg, and you could then pull that small egg apart, revealing a third egg, and a fourth, a fifth, smaller and smaller, each one more finely painted, until there were eight eggs, or nine, but what was in the last, tiny egg, as small as the nail on my pinkie, and that would remain a secret because that final egg did not come apart. It contained a mystery, Father said, a magic spell, a Finnish song, a summer's day, the footprint of a bear, the taste of a hoar-frosted berry, a halberd, a drumming shaman.

"A shama?" I asked as I held up the smallest egg to my ear.

"Shaman. A shama-a-a-a-an." Father's voice echoed, and he accompanied it with a broad gesture.

"Shaman?"

"A healer, a medium between spirits and people, a sorcerer, a dream hunter, a priest."

"A jack-of-all-trades?" I blurted, a bit too pleased with the term that came to me.

"Hmmm . . . I have new contracts with the tsardom of Muscovy." Father's voice dropped several tones. He rocked on his heels, and with a tug on his belt he straightened his leather trousers. "That's where this egg comes from. From beyond Poland. When they play their drums, they travel to other worlds."

"There, in Muscovy?"

"Only the shamans can do it. They live in the north, not far from Finnmark."

"In my school primer there's a man dressed in skins with all kinds of scraps and strings on his coat, and a crow's foot and bear teeth too. He's holding a drum. He's called a Samoyed, not a shaman."

"That's what they call the people who live there in the north."

"And they make these eggs?"

"No, it's a craft of the Russians."

"But there's a drumming shaman inside, yes?"

"Yes."

"And a summer's day?"

"Yes."

"And a song?"

"Yes."

WE DID NOT reach Cape Tabin. Far from it. But just how far off the mark we were, we had no inkling. We thought we could navigate past Novaya Zemlya, cross the Kara Sea, round what should have been Cape Tabin, and then sail on to China.

The maps made it look simple. The route was three, four, maybe even five times shorter than the route around the south, via the Cape of Good Hope, where one risked a set-to with the Portuguese or the Spaniards. No need to cross the equator, we stayed in the northern hemisphere, and if what no less an authority than Petrus Plancius claimed was true, then the North Pole was an open sea, in the summer at least, when for months the sun did not set, and the journey to India would be as easy as crossing the Zuiderzee, from Enkhuizen to Stavoren—so to speak, of course.

The North proved him wrong.

The ice proved him wrong.

And Siberia, the far deeper, endlessly sweeping forests of Siberia, proved him wrong.

The map was wrong.

If a map is inaccurate, those who trust it pay a price, the severity of which is usually proportional to that of the error in the diagram. If I disregard the toll of the two previous failed expeditions, which I might return to later, then that price was five dead: the anonymous carpenter from Purmerend who died in September, before we built the cabin, Claes Andriesz, Jan Franz, Willem Barentsz, and myself; a ship and its lost cargo: bales of velvet, linen, and baize; prints, including etchings by Bruegel, Hendrick Goltzius, and Jan Muller; a clock; and pewter tableware, such as candelabra, tankards, and saltcellars. All this to the detriment of the investors and the Emperor of China, who never got his clock; eleven frozen fingers, a few less frozen toes (the exact number is not known), and two frozen corneas. How to account for the polar bears, Arctic foxes, brent geese, gulls, and puffins captured or killed with hatchets, pickaxes, halberds, muskets, and matchlocks, I do not know. There was no bookkeeping for such matters then.

The one who paid no price at all was the draftsman himself, Petrus Plancius. He stood on the pulpit and preached. He stood on the pulpit and demonstrated the use of the astrolabe. He stood on the pulpit and cursed anyone who dared profess even a slightly more broad-minded faith than his own. This categorical expulsion of holders of contrary attitudes or beliefs was not uncommon in those days of religious profiling and civil war. He invested in what would become the voc, the Dutch East India Company. He studied the stars, made celestial globes, and had a colossal lack of insight into his own shortcomings. His intrigues, slander, and machinations made a misery of the life of the Remonstrant professor Arminius in Leiden. He produced eight children: seven sons and a daughter.

The map, in fact, was a fable. Gawain. The Round Table. The floating chessboard. But before we had caught on that the chessboard had only eight by seven rows instead of eight by eight, we were stuck in a wooden cabin clapped together with driftwood and planks from the second deck, twenty degrees below zero, on the northern tip of Novaya Zemlya.

MAPS ARE, IN part, an invitation to put the information they contain to the test. Seafarers, explorers, geographers, and adventurers accept that challenge and, if the information is too speculative, might pay for it with their life. To forgive Petrus Plancius, he was meticulous and eschewed wild conjecture, basing his work on observations and measurements made by the very finest navigators, Willem Barentsz included. A map—certainly one from the sixteenth century—wants to be put to the test.

Every map seeks a balance between too much and too little information. Superfluous content can be fatal if it distracts the person relying on the map and leads him astray.

The blank spaces on a map, where the cartographer is ignorant of the environs, can be neatly filled in with a title cartouche, a compass rose, a block of text, portraits of legendary geographers, or a detailed inset, a city map, a fantasy illustration of earthly paradise. I am likewise able, when groping in the dark, or in blankness, to turn to an exposé about the customs of the Lapps, the vegetation on Spitsbergen, the construction of the

Amsterdam canal ring, the song of a roustabout overheard in the harbor, a riddle from the *Book of Sydrac*.

How do you depict the world?

How do you depict the world on a map? Does what we call north have to be at the top? Why not the east, *ex Oriente lux*? How do you depict on a flat surface what is round and three-dimensional? What do you leave out, and what do you give extra significance by drawing it in?

How do you depict the world?

In a map, in words, in colors and forms, in music, in notes with their own duration, pitch, and volume, in dance?

How much fantasy is there in an illustration of the world?

How must a Russian pronounce "Kaap Begeerte"? Or "Orange Eylandt"? And even if a Norwegian wouldn't tie up his tongue on Spitsbergen, he makes Svalbard of it all the same. Can you blame him?

HERE I LIE, in the north of Novaya Zemlya amid driftwood, pine trunks from the great Siberian rivers, with a view of the Kara Sea, the cursed Kara Sea, aka the Karische Zee, the Karazee, or, on a map by Arnoldo di Arnoldi, "Mare Scytio"; the sea that had promised to be a gateway to the East, to porcelain, silk, and oranges, but turned out to be a wasteland of ice floes.

Here I lie, four hundred years, more than four times a hundred years, more than four times your life, here where the summer has forgotten what it is to be summer, to be sweat, fruit, ripening.

Here I lie, waiting in the ice like a mammoth's tusk nostalgic for its mammoth. In these parts where growth is slow and decay even slower. Amid the cold and the boredom of one who lives to be a thousand.

Here I lie in the forever frozen ground, which is now thawing because forever is not forever anymore.

My cells have lost none of their vitality. The images are returning. The stories are returning.

Stories inside the tiny egg that was inside a larger egg that was inside a yet larger egg, which was inside an even larger egg, and inside an egg around which was another egg with an egg around *it*, until the egg sitting in Father's open palm.

Stories in a chunk of amber, in a fly embedded in that amber, in the last thought of the fly in the amber. A dream of a summer's day and a fresh cow patty caught in a teardrop of hardened resin.

Stories, stories, images, images.

The clock ticked, the clock meant for the Emperor of China, with his daughter in rustling silk and with oranges and with palaces that smelled of sandalwood and jasmine and where you drank tea from translucent porcelain.

One day in December the clock stopped ticking. The mechanism was no match for the cold. Ice beats Emperor. Thank goodness for the sand time of the hourglass. Sand kept track of our days in the ice and snow.

If he hadn't died back in September, the carpenter could have repaired the clock. He was a born repairman. Leaky casks, frayed ropes, torn sailcloth, metalwork come loose from sea chests, the compass when it went haywire. He wove me a hammock, because all I had brought with me were some clothes, a blanket, my writing kit, and books. Once, he refastened the damaged rudder. Four other times he disappeared into the depths of the ship with a hammer and nails. In calmer periods, while the other sailors washed their clothes and laid them out on the deck to dry, he made ships in bottles. Just before his death, he told us how to build a log cabin, should we be forced to spend the winter on land. We were to use whole tree trunks, and place their ends crosswise over each other—this building technique came to him during the journey. He had gotten the clock ticking again, even with temperatures far below zero.

Zero is a dream in the polar night.

Zero is a faraway summer.

Zero is a fever dream.

Zero does not exist in the polar night.

Here I lie amid errant winds making their way across frozen seas. Here where there is no tree or shrub to protect you from the elements. Where the wind is more tangible than a piece of fruit.

There's been rumbling recently. A strange kind of pressure. Reverberations. Gas bubbles form and dissolve, but then new gas bubbles well up. The bubbles sound like the bells of a drowned city.

This is the warmth they predicted.

This is time doing its work on the eternal ice.

It grimaces, has pointy ears and yellow pupils.

"Brrots," time belches.

"IN THE BLUE blue ocean," Grandmother said, "a whale swims, and in the hollow hollow belly of the whale, a man sits at a table by the light of a whale oil lamp and writes on a sheet in a book, on a sheet of parchment—paper, as you know, won't hold up against the digestive juices of a whale. He writes on a sheet of whale skin about a cold blue ocean, about a whale with a man in its belly, who writes by the light of a whale oil lamp about, you've guessed it already, the cold ocean, a whale, and a book, and whoever finds this book will, he will, what will he? Live forever? Dig up a pot of gold in his backyard? What do you think? Will he discover the island of eternal happiness? Or live in a house with a roof made of pancakes? That is what's written in the book of the man who writes by the light of a whale oil lamp on a sheet, a sheet of whale skin in the belly of a whale in the blue blue ocean. The End. And now to bed, my little dreamer. To bed. Dream, dream of the book and tell me tomorrow what's in it."

IN THE SIXTEENTH century, the boundaries of the known world changed with nearly every ship that returned from a long voyage. Even the "coasters"—the coastal merchant ships—provided plenty of useful knowledge if they had an observant, inquisitive pilot on board. Meteorologists, geographers, astronomers, and assorted stargazers would analyze the new information. Mapmakers and engravers collated the data, ideas, and speculations and incorporated them into new maps, which in turn provoked debate, put minds to work, prompted treatises, and gave birth to new theories, which were subsequently disproven by the next ship returning from the East Indies.

I enjoyed my sixteenth century. I saw it all evolve: man rebelling against doctrines and oppressors, man casting off his yoke and donning a new coat more suited to his knowledge-hungry time. It was not destructive energy but enthusiasm, perhaps also a naive openness for innovative ideas, the will to test, and extend, boundaries with ingenious techniques and newfangled instruments. I also saw the signs of the inevitable hardening: the dominant belief had its own dogmas, its own executioners. Moderation and tolerance made way for fanaticism and intransigence.

Later, you could see how dogmas always start as part of a doctrine, and are not in small measure responsible for its success.

Later, one becomes more reconciled with the intransigence of those who are convinced they know what is true and what isn't.

But I never could fathom why it's so difficult to allow a wealth of differences to coexist. What good is harmony without diversity?

I wouldn't have missed the sixteenth century for any amount of gold, which had come over by the shipful from the New World. This was the century that began in 1492 and had to come to terms with the discovery of a continent that was not mentioned in a single book of the Bible. My contemporaries did so by simply continuing to discover.

The *mappae mundi* of Gemma Frisius, Mercator, Ortelius, and Jodocus Hondius, published by Plantijn in Antwerp, Jan Seversz in Leiden, or Cornelis Claesz in Amsterdam, were outdated before they even went to press. The telescope peered deep into the heavens. Tycho Brahe was given his own private island, Hven, in the Sont, to build his observatory, Uraniborg. The microscope would later reveal a universe in a grain of sand.

My fellow poets at the De Egelantier rhetorical society went green with envy over my crocodile-skin gloves. I flapped my bleached-white lace cuffs, theatrically exposing my gloved hands, before taking a swig of Asti Spumante and launching into a drinking song. Amsterdam brimmed with expectation, whirred with activity. Broad-bellied ships heading to and from exotic destinations and foreign markets; colorful foreigners fleeing religious tyranny, bringing with them finesse and knowledge; languages, words, and idioms ripe for translation.

In short, the city was abuzz, and I was a child of my time.

THE SEA CRACKLED from the ice, within it a faraway, faintly tingling sigh. From even farther or deeper rose a dark rumbling, as though from an underworld.

White wisps of water vapor hung like balloons in front of our blue, chafed lips. Close your eyes, and your lashes froze together. Four of us lugged a tree trunk, and the rope cut through three layers of felt into our aching shoulders.

An ice field is not flat. It is a rugged landscape of ice and snow, with ridges, fissures, crevasses, razor-sharp protrusions, impassable dams, irregularly jutting plateaus. Dragging logs across an ice field is a strongman contest at a carnival.

We had to lean back and dig in our heels, but by then we were too weak to put any real force behind it. A leg would slip sideways, we'd sink up to our knees in a snow hollow, we'd stagger over a crumbling ridge; feet slipped every which way, the ground disappeared, and we stepped onto thin air, nearly falling over but only just managing to keep hold of the rope.

Jacob Evertsz cursed, and the curse froze in midair before it had even finished sounding, and without reaching a single ear it fell and landed on the ice with a plunk, like the Devil's turd.

Brrots!

The air was so cold that you could bite it into pieces. You bit into it, and the cold shot straight to your forehead, pressed against your eyeballs, and your jaw contracted, making your teeth creak like they were about to crack. Then, after some time, you took another bite. Elsewhere they call this breathing. But what this here was, no one knew.

Soon enough, I was too weak to drag logs. But one morning I had the energy to do a round of the traps. When you opened the door, the stony-cold breath of an icehouse whipped you in the face. It was quiet outside, a sign of mist. I fumbled for the rope to tie around my waist, the other end fastened to the cabin. This way you could lose all sense of direction—hardly even being able to tell up from down—amid the total whiteness that dissolved into the horizon, and still find your way back.

But first you had to get the door to open. I heaved my shoulder against it with what little weight I still had. The door gave slowly, with a dignified calm, as though inviting me outside with much ceremonious and needless delay.

A velvety breath grazed my face, like the fur of a pelted animal. Such an idyllic scene. The new day after a night of snowfall. A tranquil winter morning. The world pure and white. The snow pristine, save the spoor of an Arctic fox. The sparkling ice floes in the bay, floating alongside one another in attractive patterns.

The glittering play of crystals and shimmering snow stars. A world as close to death as to the onset of life.

The sky was high and endless. My gaze drifted across the soothing whiteness. It was like a mirage, a fata morgana, or the dream of the Arctic fox that had passed over this expanse of snow during the night.

I could have stepped into the hibernation of a polar bear.

I was surprised by how dry snow could be, dry and compact.

Even during a calamity like ours, there are moments of beauty and wonder. They can be idyllic or fearsome and grotesque, but they accompany us, these moments, they nudge us knowingly, and in a blink, they're gone.

Sometimes that blink would inspire a poem in me. Not that it was much, despite all my literary bravura. I was not a prolific writer. But if I put my mind to it, I only had to shake the tree and the fruit fell into my lap. Or have I said this already? Shadows of a wink from another world. Sometimes it is a song that is sung generation after generation.

Thus travels a blink or a moment through time.

As a poem.

As a song.

As a myth.

The Arctic fox walked his nightly route, sniffed the bait, dug with his forepaws, found the scraps of fish, and the snow held back the trap.

I took hold of a shovel.

It was my last day outside.

ON THE OTHER side, a walrus was waiting for me. He told me about the All and the One and the One in the All and the All in the One. He stripped off his hide and tusked mask and welcomed me with a polar-bear hug. During the embrace the polar bear, too, shed his hide. What was left was a scraggy little Arctic fox, who rubbed up against my shin so that his fur peeled off as well. From the Arctic fox leaped a snow hare, just as a snow-white hare escaped from my chest and, leaping, melted into the hare that ran in a straight line toward the horizon.

NOVAYA ZEMLYA—WE eventually made it that far. Not beyond the point that should have opened onto the passage to Cathay—not that bunkum, the arena of approval-needy geographers or feverish, greedy tradesmen—no, the point beyond which no friendship can exist, not even the fairy tale of the coyest fondness, the point beyond which it's just you and the polar night, the point beyond which you only snarl orders and glower coldly at one another. No spices, no tea, porcelain, silk, fragrant nutmeg or cloves, not a single pepper, only the void, the immeasurable void where every man is on his own in the endless polar whiteness. This void, I, that is to say, we—the barber Hans Vos, Laurens Willemsz, Pieter Pietersz Vos, Jacob Evertsz, Jacob Jansz Sterrenburgh, and a few more such names—understood, is everywhere, even before Novaya Zemlya, but you have to reach Novaya Zemlya to realize this. Novaya Zemlya is everywhere. Novaya Zemlya is everything. I stayed behind in the polar night, the sun was a mirage, I did not join the journey in open sloops back along Novaya Zemlya's west coast and the north coast of Russia until the White Sea, where Jan Cornelisz

Rijp's rescue ship had dropped anchor. My voice comes from the polar night, from a hibernation lasting four centuries, from the void of four hundred years of ice, ice, and more ice. There is no one to share the bottomless void with. No one. *no one!* Understood?

I RECOGNIZED MYSELF in an Arctic fox. A rogue, scrouging and scavenging across the tundra, fur trembling with melancholy and a hint of guile on his grinning maw.

My commission was to compose an ode to the presumed, despite the odds, success of the mission. To the sound judgment of the Admiralty of Amsterdam—or was it the city council, a tradesmen's guild? (after four hundred years, you get things jumbled up)—to kit out a new northern fleet; to that eminent geographer, Petrus Plancius; to the leadership and wisdom of the captain, our skipper, Jacob van Heemskerck; to the sublime navigating skills, second to none, as everyone well knew, of Willem Barentsz; to the most exalted Emperor of China and the friendship between his illustrious empire and the Netherlands, Amsterdam in particular.

My disdain for my patrons aside, it should have been an easy task. On the aforementioned map of Novaya Zemlya there is, on the west coast, a bluff named Cape Plancius. I needn't take it any further than that. My alexandrines stood at the ready; from Virgil I had plucked the sour berries the

Scythians used to make their wine; from Herodotus I had learned the art of description; I had poked around Quintilian so as to spice up my style with rhetorical devices. I had only to toss in enough invigorating details: names of cities, envoys, local folkloric customs, a few words of dialect—a guaranteed success—weather conditions, a bit of chitchat with a passerby while surveying the land, a solitary fisherman, the blunt talk of a harbormaster. It had to include a storm, naturally, and a miraculous rescue. I found sea monsters in Adriaen Coenen's *Fish Book* and *Whale Book*. Terms like ice drift, topsail wind, north-northeast, ice heaves, and compass needle could wait for the cadence to determine their place. I would generously sprinkle it with words like valiant, intrepid, stouthearted, hardship, steadfast, fearless, proud, and audacious. Later I would add the spices and smells, the textiles and tastes of China.

But not a word about the folly of the venture.

And so it went, even after me.

With odes to ships that set sail from Middelburg to Ghana, from there to Brazil or Guyana or Curaçao, and then back to Middelburg.

What a palaver just to measure the three sides of a triangle.

But now I know the statistics.

Now I am aware of the cargo, that so-called "ebony": wood no lumberman traded and which Father would have scowled at.

You must, as Petrus Plancius never tired of saying, determine your position. The Sint-Nicolaaskerk, named for the patron saint of mariners, became the Oude Kerk once the Protestants kicked the Catholics out.

I have seen much.
I can see far.
There is much I can tell.

SO AS NOT to draw attention to myself, I was not listed on the muster roll by name. I was passed off as an interpreter or deputy trade clerk, or as an aide to an envoy to the Tsardom of Muscovy who was not even on board. My alias, which circulated in various guises—I was alternately Bartolomeo, Loo, Arto, Tolomeo, Lome, and, even to those who believed I had something to do with construction projects in China, Bartolucci—evaporated after my death, so thin was my identity, like one last sigh in the polar night. Mention must be made of the punctilious clerk in some labyrinthine building, who in 1597 scratched my fabricated name from the muster roll and, to frustrate future researchers even more, also erased the name of the carpenter, as well as the names of the ships themselves. Since then, I have been known as "anonymous crewman"—a blessed state for a poet, especially a dead one.

Nothing of me has been saved except for two lines of verse which, foreseeing the later Romantic practice, I carved on a wooden beam in the Behouden Huys. After my fifteen fellow crewmen left in June 1597, time took its toll on the cabin.

That is, snow, wind, frost, and storms dismembered the hut, an anomaly in that landscape, into its separate elements, and thus the trunk on which I had scratched my distich found its way during a spring storm to the Kara Sea, into which the Yenisey River had dumped it—I nearly said dumped "me"—thirty years earlier.

How the beam made it through waters more often frozen than not, meandering along the north of Siberia, through the Bering Strait, and into the Pacific Ocean, is an adventure that only Nordenskiöld, the explorer who did find the Northeast Passage, but only in 1878, can relate. Here it will suffice to report that my literary legacy washed up on the shores of Alaska and once again—perhaps as a distant echo of my youthful ambition to become an architect—became part of the wall of a log cabin, for some time the bivouac of a poacher and, later, a shelter for hikers caught unawares by blizzards.

In those years, somewhere in the course of the nineteenth century, the beam—my beam—caught the eye of a Dutch-speaking Canadian; he'd learned from his grandmother with the unusual surname Duesseron. He copied the lines into his best-loved book, Alexander von Humboldt's *Views of Nature*, translated them into English, and showed them to a poet friend, who then wove a terrible epos around them. One strophe from it, containing my couplet, would, however, in turn inspire another poet to write an audacious, intensely passionate song of I, I, myself, being, leaves of grass, and more I. Signed: Arto, Loo, Tolo, aka Bartolomeo.

There is another, albeit less plausible, variant. In the interest of thoroughness, however, I will share it here so that you can decide for yourself which version you choose to believe, whereby it must also be said that both versions could be true—in my own environs, that is, not in your world bounded by time and space.

Now the beam does not drift eastward but against the current to the west, where it rounds the North Cape, bobs southward, nearly gets dragged to the seabed in the maelstrom between Å and Værøy, but just as miraculously escapes from the vortex, shoots across the North Sea, and, with playful ease, passes the cross waves of the English Channel to wash ashore, sometime in the second half of the seventeenth century, on the coast of Portugal. There, the beam is sawed into planks that a potter uses to build a dog kennel, but not before making a wax imprint of the now worn-down words. That wax tablet sits in his atelier, collecting dust, until his great-grandson uses the text as an exotic motif for a vase. And, well, how this vase played an essential mnemotechnical role in the poetic awakening of a commercial correspondent in a night of dozens or even hundreds of poems is already sufficiently known, yet without the source of those two lines ever having been established.

It is up to you which of the two versions to believe.

The best part is that as long as you remain here in my domain, it doesn't matter which you choose.

THIS IS AN excellent place for a cartouche, in the form of an insert, an explanation. I've mentioned the word "Samoyed" a number of times. The child I was had a primer—a picture book with illustrations of a profession, an object, a nation or folk, a conveyance, a building, and each illustration was accompanied by a description in Latin, English, German, and Dutch—and read the word "Samoyed" alongside a man dressed in a woolly pelt, holding a bow and arrow. Behind him, a similar-looking man sat on a sled pulled by reindeer. It came up in the conversation I had with my father in connection with the egg that contained an egg that also contained an egg and so on, until a tiny inseparable egg was left over that held, among many other things, a Finnish song, the colors of autumn, the quiet leap of a fish, the surprise of a snail, rain, a damaged spiderweb, and a shaman's drum dance.

For the sake of convenience, I will quote a text insert from an old map: "The world 'Samoyed' (Samoyeds, pl.) requires explanation. In older references to these northern peoples, the name's roots are traced to the Russian words for 'self' (сам) and 'eat' {едим [yedim] (we eat), еда (n.) [yeda] (food)}, thus to self-eater, i.e., cannibal. More likely, however, is that the word originated from the Lapp 'samoyedne,' meaning 'land of the Sami,' or 'land of the Lapps.'

"'Samoyed' is an obsolete term for what are in fact three distinct peoples: the Nganasans, the Enets, and the Nenets. The Samoyedic people, with whom expeditions preceding ours exchanged information—for better or worse—were Nenets. They lived in the far north of Russia, their territory extending from the east of Arkhangelsk to the west of Taymyr. They likely migrated northward between 1100 and 1400 from more southern parts along the Siberian Rivers Ob and Yenisey. There, they adopted the fishing and sailing techniques of a hitherto unknown folk. Nenets, like Russian fishermen, were aware of Novaya Zemlya and the Kara Sea coasts long before these were 'discovered' by Borough and Barentsz."

A cartouche-within-the-cartouche will inform the reader that forty years prior to Willem Barentsz & Co., Stephen Borough, on behalf of the Muscovy Company, sailed to the northeast with the aim of locating the River Ob, on whose banks lived devotees of Zlota Baba, the goddess of wealth. This "Zlota," derived from the Russian золото [zoloto] and золотая [zolotaya], or "gold" (n.) and "golden" (adj.), promised to be an avenue of wealth. Borough got no farther than Novaya Zemlya, but discovered for Western European seamen and traders not only this island but the strait leading to the Kara Sea.

HIS SERMON HAD started out convincingly enough. About God's order. He articulated the "d" and the "s" in such a way that a barely audible "e" emerged between them, more an "uh" sound, so that "God's" would reverberate nicely without him actually adding an extra syllable. The intention was that "God's" appeared to have elongated itself and resounded thanks to its own unfathomable depth; this echo was meant to capture the point of his sermon, namely the complete transcendence of God's order, against which every human inclination would crumble, or in which it would dissolve. Petrus Plancius paused. Everything was written in the books; his discourse continued—and there he suddenly lost his place. The Portuguese ship's journals popped into his head. Again. They had been invaluable to the sailing instructions he had drawn up for de Houtman. Should the northern route fail, then around the south. In the next sentence he remarked on the blessing of precise orientation. Someone in the fourth row cleared his throat. Plancius picked up the thread, or so he thought, by drawing an elegant parallel between the cartographer and the Creator. He spoke of leaving port and orientation, about returning home and finding harbors. About true faith being a safe haven. The cartographer had the divine power *and*—pause, emphasis, the pause mustn't last too long, the rhetorical device shouldn't be obvious, it should be a natural-sounding pause, pensive, casting about for the right word—the responsibility to bring order between the sacred and the profane. Yes, that was it, he was on the right track. The civilized and the savage, the secure and the lawless. And suddenly he was standing on the pulpit, holding an astrolabe. Where did that come from? He had left the instrument at home, he was sure of it, lessons were only tomorrow, also in a church, another one, true, but never on a Sunday. The astrolabe was capable of immense computing power. The position of the sun and the stars, the height of a tower or the depth of a well—yes, *that* well from Genesis, Joseph, Johannes, which of them was it again who got thrown into the cistern?, the white fish in the cistern, yes, that was a good lead-in, you just have to spot it, then you see everything, everything in a single image, in a note, and then you're the one who is touched and the fish speaks to you—the movement of the planets, the liturgical calendar, the calculation of Easter, the monastic prayers. There were no secrets behind this monstrance-like—those Catholics again, bah!—object that Petrus Plancius held up to his congregation. How one held the astrolabe, tilted upward and at arm's length, pointed at the sun or a star, how the light shone through a pair of pinholes in the rotating indicator, or "rete," onto the back plate, the "tympan," which then revealed a wealth of information that finds its way to star charts, moon charts, tabular handbooks, yearly calendars. "It's all about orientation,"

Plancius said, sweaty and exhausted, grasping at his trusted *idée fixe* to rescue himself. He was teetering. He had to stay the course; orientation was the correct path. The only one. The true one. Orientation. Longitudinal orientation. No, not longitudinal orientation. Jacobus Arminius in Leiden misses the point because he's taken the wrong path. Because he has veered off from the Word. Orientation, orientation—you must be able to orient yourself. Those freethinking Remonstrants are unable to. They jumble up everything. All that leads to is a blurring of terms, blurring of positions. Blight that corrupts the holy edifice from the inside out. Worse than, than, well, than . . . than those Catholic malcontents . . . Bubbles of saliva formed in the corners of his mouth. If anyone here, *anyone* . . . but he did not finish his threat. In the back of his thoughts—or was it there behind the pillar, where a dog lifted its leg and began to piss, or was it there in the fourth row?—a goblin appeared, doing handstands and somersaults while making ludicrous faces. A grimacing, diabolical mug with a pockmarked nose, pointed ears, and bloodshot eyes with yellow pupils. Plancius grasped the copper instrument, not the flat astrolabium catholicum , the universal astrolabe of Professor Frisius in Leuven, but the Arabic instrument over which Adelard of Bath had written.

WE SAILED INTO a fjord, and at the end it opened onto another fjord, narrow with steep cliffs that radiated coolness, and when we decided to moor, yet another fjord appeared behind a bluff, this one lined with green rolling hills, so that we did not drop anchor after all but kept sailing until a headland jutted out, narrowing the passage so much that we were forced to reef the sails and proceed slowly, like mulling over a thought, but when we approached the headland, we saw a sound that gave us access to a bay with sandy banks and green, thickly wooded hillsides, and there we moored.

I MARVELED AT the maps on the walls in the bookshop on Amsterdam's Warmoesstraat: *mappae mundi*, compass maps, contours of barely discovered continents, town plans, coastlines, the Øresund, the Baltic Sea with all its port cities, names like Riga, Reval, Stettin, Vyborg, Lübeck and Gdańsk (on one map), Danzig (on another, and also Gidanic and Gdancyk) roused my fantasy. Outside on the cart there were travel journals, atlases for pilots, almanacs, portolan charts, treatises on navigation and longitude orientation.

For me, the sea itself held not the least allure, but a world captured in a grid of parallels and meridians aroused my fascination, the suggestive combination of precision and abstraction, exactitude and expression, as if a map were a box of building blocks ready to be assembled as you wished. I wandered through a forest of land maps, floated over globes, and traced constellations. I got to know a folk described in a cartouche, learned about spices, minerals, exotic fruits, shells, tortoises. I held the universe in my hands.

If lyrical rapture had not drawn me to nomadic, open-air life, I would have studied to be an architect. I pictured myself hunched over a draftsman's table, designing structures with compass and ruler, creating spaces within larger ones, inventing worlds by connecting points and lines just like on those maps, globes, and, later, atlases. I spent a fortune on *De architectura* by Vitruvius, inquired with Hendrik Laurensz Spieghel at De Egelantier after an architect he knew, went to Leuven to see what the university there had to offer—but my Jewish mentor had only to describe the life of traveling and writing, and I gave in to my urge to sing.

On the bookshop's counter, in addition to a globe, there were inkpots, a jar of goose quills, sticks of bloodred sealing wax, scraping knives, playing cards, and, in a box lined with green-and-gold-striped cotton, samples of diverse kinds of paper. A tempting aroma wafted from a dish with nougat, sweets, and candied ginger.

The bookseller leaned against a cabinet and watched me; his gaze followed my moves as though it were a magic wand that tapped me, awakening in me something unknown, pure, a sort of springtime, a lust for life. A world that hesitantly emerged from the darkness, its contours sleepily soft.

The dusty light fell upon the book press, an astrolabe, the book blocks waiting to be bound, a stack of Maarten van Heemskerck engravings; it shone obliquely along the cubbyholes holding rolls of cotton, satin, and leather.

From the bookshop I hurried to the lumberyards on the east side of the city. There, a carpenter acquaintance whom Father supplied with wood had his workplace. The fresh scent of wet bark hung in the air; saws sang their way effortlessly through the logs.

So, a few years before I boarded Willem Barentsz's ship for that cursed journey to the North that was supposed to bring us in record time to the East, I made my way through the lumberyards and timber basins, past the shipyards with their intoxicating smell of tar, to this carpenter on whose lap I sat when I was still in britches.

Amsterdam was built on wood; in fact, its prosperity itself was indebted to wood, the wood of the trading ships. The fledgling golden age was an age of wood and smelled, appropriately, of rosin and fresh bark. The saws never stopped sawing.

"Apparently there's a mill in Uitgeest that saws tree trunks," I said to the carpenter. His hands were caked with sawdust, and when he ran his fingers through his silver-gray hair, the powder stuck to his hair and his ear. And in his eyebrows.

"It'll never work."

"I heard it from a lumberman, and on the Oude Brug they were talking about it too."

"A mill will never saw as accurately as a man, let alone as cleanly as a carpenter. If you don't follow the fibers, you'll ruin the wood, and then it's useless."

He scratched his cheek with a wood shaving. "They'll say anything these days. Now they're even talking about sailing to the Indies via Norway."

The carpenter shook his head and ran his fingers along a beam he had been planing when I arrived.

"There must be something to those sawmills," I said. "Why else would the Amsterdam guild want to forbid them?"

"They're scared, that's why! Those fellows in charge shit themselves at the slightest provocation. Who would want a fancy cabinet, a spinet, a bed made by wood sawed by a mill? Pfff. Let the mills pound piles, grind grain, or pump water. Let them even saw wood, but then for troughs, not for a ship that's going to transport a fortune."

"No other news?" I ran my hand through a small heap of wood curls and let the shavings fall back through my fingers onto the pile.

"Yes, or no, no news . . . You know, when you used to come here with your pa, you said wood could sing. Every trunk—you heard its voice. You even sang what it sounded like. Brazilwood, you used to love that, remember? Did we laugh. A child's fantasy . . . Did we laugh! But you know, in a way you were right. A saw can make a tree trunk sing. You don't need to use force to find the line through the wood. Better not to, in fact. What brute would entrust his wood to a mill?"

MY FATHER RETURNED from his trips to Poland and Finland with gifts. For my mother, lacquered boxes with glistening inlays, clothes with white needlework trim, sometimes a piece of jewelry. For me, toys: always a new kind of spinning top with ingenious color patterns that spun into new colors, sometimes even leaping to patterns, so it was more like a spectacle of light than an ordinary wooden cone. Father brought a whiff of woods and wilderness with him, and with it, stories, riddles, or a magic trick.

"What's the most precious stone?" he once asked. In his sparkling eyes and that trace of mockery on his mouth, I could already sense a trick question was afoot. He had just given me a honey-colored, translucent stone, a glass-like substance with a fly trapped inside it. "This is solidified resin," Father explained, "and the fly, lured by the sweetness of the pine sap, got stuck in the gold-brown gunk."

This amber was not the answer to Father's question; at most it had inspired the riddle. Partly to play along, partly because I knew I would never get the real answer if I didn't hazard a few wrong guesses first, I cried, "A ruby!"

"Why a ruby, now?" Father asked. The irritation in his voice surprised even me.

"Red can be everything. Hate and love. Fire and brick. Blood and lava."

"No."

Not that I had expected a different reply. But I stuck with the gemstones, even though I knew I was on the wrong track.

"Sapphire."

"No."

"It's a nice word."

"But it's not the answer."

"Topaz—it comes in many colors."

Father shook his head.

"Emerald." I thought of Samuel Ben Yohai's green eyes. He had just given me two collections of poetry from Al-Andalus. He spoke of Al-Andalus with melancholy and with pride. Damascius, with his smirk and ironic snicker, questioned everything; he taught by doubt. Ben Yohai, on the other hand, taught us with a gentle smile in his eyes, bathing his students in a mild glow.

"Not that either."

I pouted theatrically and shrugged.

"A stone that's useful to everyone."

It was probably obvious, which is why I couldn't think of it. That's how it is with riddles. We do not see what is in front of our nose. This was in front of my nose.

"Millstones. They grind everyone's grain."

The words had hardly left Father's mouth when he pulled a playing card from his shirtsleeve: king of spades. He put it in his vest pocket, did a circuit of the room, stopping to run his fingers over the keys of the spinet, bent over, and pulled the card from his right bootleg.

"Pay attention, and you'll figure it out."

"The card was already in your shoe," I exclaimed.

He fanned out a deck of cards. "Pick one."

I held out the three of diamonds.

"No, don't let me see it. Another one."

Now I picked the queen of diamonds.

Father put the card face down into his mouth, chewed, swallowed, walked through the room, played another run on the spinet, and pulled a card from the pocket of his coat that was draped over the chair: queen of diamonds.

"Pay attention, and you'll figure it out."

Meanwhile, his rafts of timber, six layers thick, drifted down the Dniester, Pripyat, Oder, Vistula, Elbe, bobbed across a Finnish lake, were lashed together to form ever-longer, snaking rafts, sometimes hundreds of meters long, until they reached a Baltic Sea harbor or perhaps a Black Sea one and were loaded into the hold of a ship, or, no, floated farther, farther along the Rhine.

WE SAW A fountain.

We saw dancing mist.

Jacob Jansz Hooghwout crossed himself. “A whale,” he said to himself, “a whale.” He saw a whale. Never mind that he betrayed himself as a Catholic, he tossed in a couple of Hail Marys and arrow prayers for good measure. A whale—he had seen a whale, as big as a ballroom, although he had never seen one of these before either. All right then, as big as a cathedral, this he had seen once, from a distance, in some harbor or another, maybe Lisbon or Genoa or Marseille; he would tell his wife once he was back on Ameland, and his daughters, Stien and Vosje, too. Papa saw a whale, it was as big as a palace, and this would shut up Gilbert, his smug brother-in-law in Leeuwarden, from now on; he had some job at the secretariat and boasted every time they saw each other, fortunately not too often, that once, when he was on Vlieland on court business, God knows what for, he had seen a beached sperm whale. Gilbert always related this with an insufferable air of importance.

Jacob Jansz Hooghwout saw a whale. Laurens Willemsz saw a whale. Willem Barentsz saw a whale. Jacob van Heemskerck saw a whale. Some, legend has it, saw a forest on the whale's smooth back. One man, Pieter Cornelisz I think it was, claimed to see a monk, but a fifth or sixth deckhand shouted, "A monk *and* a forest! A monk *in* a forest! He's writing in a book." This was the senses pushed to excess, dulled by days of sailing through mist as thick as gruel, by eyes overexerted and exhausted from endless staring into white and gray and gray white and white gray. If some object comes into view—an ice floe, another ship, a gull or an albatross, or, like now, a whale—one's stimulus-starved perception pounces on any minimal contrast with the gray, embellishes it, frantically searching for something to grasp on to, with fugitive memories, fearful visions, fantasies long in storage. But this I can tell you: there was no forest, there was no monk writing in a book; it was the oval-shaped back of a whale, onto which the seamen projected their fear and their desires.

Our diligent scribe, too, was haunted for days by visions his exhausted eyes had showed him, but he was wise enough not to write them down. Or else he redacted them later, aware of the dustup that awaited him for his report of having seen the sun two weeks earlier than Scala's *Almanac* predicted it. And a dustup it was too. Gerrit de Veer was subjected to a scientific interrogation, only to be dismissed as a fantasist who had seen a sun where there was no sun to be seen. And still, I saw it, he had mumbled. Kepler later proved him right, albeit with the qualification that it was not the sun itself he had seen, but a reflection of it.

The obliging scribe and disciple of Willem Barentsz—who conscientiously and dutifully kept a daily journal, notating our course and the weather conditions, even when we had three consecutive days of sun and not a puff of wind or when we went ashore—left those days of his bewilderment blank, and rightly so. You will find in the *Waerachtighe Beschryvinghe van Drie Seylagien, ter Werelt Noyt Soo Vreemt Ghehoort* not a single entry for July 22 through 29, 1596, nor in the German edition, aside from an offhand, trivial, distracting comment regarding bleaching shirts and carving crosses.

Some spoke of having seen a forest on the back of a whale, as legend has it, others saw a monk, and the one who saw the monk sitting in a floating forest writing in a book even claimed he could read what the monk wrote.

Jacob Jansz Hooghwout crossed himself; he did not have to indulge in fantasies, for, being loyal to the Mother Church, he knew a miracle when he saw one. That the others had seen a forest on the whale's back, well, let legend be legend. Another one had babbled about seeing a monk writing—as though it weren't enough to see a whale! A whale. Leviathan! Yes, that is what he would say, he had seen Leviathan, not a whale, no, Leviathan; otherwise, his brother-in-law would surely ask, "What kind of whale, then?" and he had to be a step ahead of Gilbert. Leviathan.

WE ALL CHASE after Novaya Zemlya visions, distorted reflections of the true light, with no compass but our expectations, which blur the view and make us lose our bearings.

We live in a landscape of dreams. Barrenness or abundance is not gauged by the number of plant or animal species, by the sum total of the flora and fauna, nor by human endeavors; it is the dreams, memories, stories, and legends that lend the landscape its intensity and radiance.

If we do not dream, tell stories, cultivate memories, then our surroundings—whether a bustling city or a mountain valley, an island on the crossroads of trading routes or a speck of half a dozen houses on the far side of an impenetrable wood—will be bare and nonviable.

Here I am, buried in the frozen ground of northern Novaya Zemlya. Here, where what shines like gold is not gold but pyrite, where the White Honeyeater—Russian for polar bear—does not crave honey but hunts seals, where there is no tree or shrub to protect you from the elements. I've been lying here for four hundred years in icy silence, but I have always traveled farther, about cold villages.

Novaya Zemlya is my everything.

Novaya Zemlya is my ruin.

Novaya Zemlya is my salvation.

For a few decades now, the atmosphere here has been uneasy. Edgy. Things aren't what they used to be: the contours are fluid, one thing becomes the other, the other becomes the one that is a different one than the one at the beginning and then is no longer one but two or three, five, six, eight, or whatever you please.

Come now, great warmth, warmth that can make centuries of frost flow into a stream of words. My words have been frozen for too long. Four times a hundred years, I've watched geese fly overhead, four times a hundred years in the brief—far too brief—spring, four times a hundred years in the early autumn, four times a hundred years, I have heard their call without being able to greet them back.

Come now, Great Thaw that will melt the centuries-long frost, and will let my words flow.

Come, warmth, come!

GRANDMOTHER BEGAN TELLING a story. It was when we lived in the low house with the thatched roof, where she grew beans, rapeseed, and turnips, even a few rows of spelt. Her words beaded up like air bubbles in the burbling water from a spring. “I know something else,” she said. “‘I know something else,’ the hen said to the fox. ‘Well, I know even more,’ the fox replied. He had the hen clamped in his jaw and was just about to take a bite.

“‘How graceful your posture is. So dignified. But your father could do it better,’ said the hen,” said Grandmother, in a pinched, high-pitched voice, like she was struggling for air.

“‘Oh, really?’

“‘Whenever he caught me, he would close his left eye.’

“‘Ohhh, I can do that.’

“‘First-rate! And so dignified, how you’re sitting. Very good. But your father could do it better.’

“‘How so?’ said the fox,” said Grandmother, with a voice shrill with surprise.

“‘Your father also closed his right eye.’

“‘Ohhh, I can do that too.’

"'The spitting image of your father, with your eyes closed, and your pointy snout, your gleaming teeth. But your father could do it better.'

"'How so?'

"'So as to be more relaxed while he ate, he would put his paws behind his neck.'

"'Ohhh, I can do that too.'

"'Excellent! And so elegant. Couldn't be better. Or, actually, there was more your father could do.'

"'Oh? What, then?'

"'Before he took a bite, he always counted to ten. He'd learned that from his father. He didn't teach you that?'

"'I don't need my father to teach me that. One, two—' And off flew the hen, into the nearest tree."

Grandmother closed her eyes and smiled silently. Before she would go on, I always had to ask, "Granny, what else do you know?" And still she kept quiet. It seemed like she shut her eyes even tighter, but I knew from her smile that she would tell me more.

"I know more. The fox begged the hen to come down from the tree. He would not hurt her; he only wanted to hear more about his father.

"'All right, if you insist,' said the hen. 'Wait, I see someone off in the distance.'

"'What? Who?' asked the fox. 'I can't tell for sure, but he's got a rifle.' And the fox took off like a shot."

A man did come along, not a hunter but a hawker who walked with a limp, leaning on a crutch made of a smoothed-out oak branch. His willow-twig basket revealed an array of merchandise: wooden spoons, cups, mousetraps, bobbins. Also something that resembled a miniature wooden pitchfork.

"What is that for?" Grandmother asked.

"They use it in Brabant."

"Do the frogs pitch hay there?"

"It's to eat with."

"To eat with?"

"They sell like hotcakes. Keeps their fine hands clean."

"Or they don't dirty their fine food," Grandmother said with a sneer.

"They wash with soap."

"With the Devil's dreck, you mean."

She drew water from the well, gave the tired, pale man cheese, bread, eggs, and a sausage in exchange for two mousetraps.

"At the next crossing, an hour's walk from here, you mustn't stop to rest in the shade of the hazel trees, and don't eat their nuts."

"Why not?"

"An evil spirit lives there. At midnight you can hear wailing and howling. It's enough to scare you stiff. Yammerer's Corner, it's called."

"Nonsense, auntie. You want to keep those nuts for yourself."

"Only a simpleton does not know what he should know."

"There's a hole in my coat pocket. The day falls through it, and I chase after it."

"You're welcome to play the fool, but it won't do you any good . . . Stay clear of the hazels. Take it from me. Elderberry works against squabbling. Here, take this bunch so you don't forget my words."

The next day they found the hawker dead under the hazel trees, with a burn mark in the hollow of his chest.

Grandmother sat plucking a goose that she held between her knees, its head dangling on the slack neck.

"Granny, Granny, what else do you know?"

THE BOATS LOOKED as if they sailed straight through the bridges across the Damrak, through the Nieuwe Brug, the Oude Brug, where Father met tradesmen, and with just as much ease through the Papenbrug, as though the bridge wasn't even there.

Cleverly, a loose plank had been removed from the middle of the bridge deck, just wide enough to let the mast through.

The smells varied, from the soap from the boilery and the sea of the fish stalls on the sluice to the forest from the wet tree bark and sap from the nearby lumberyards. But just as penetrating was the stench coming from the canals.

On the streets and alleys on either side of Dam Square, cabinetmakers, bakers, weavers, goldsmiths, and cobblers had their shops and workplaces, with the corresponding smells and activity. Tanners folded down the front shutters of their workshops into shelves displaying leather bags, belts, gloves, money pouches, sometimes a saddlebag, even a whip.

In an alley leading to the Geldersekade, near a chandler, I often stopped to watch a glassblower. A glowing orange-golden sphere hung on the end of his long pipe. The heat stung my face—I could not fathom how the man with the pipe in his mouth could stand being so close to the oven. His face and hands glistened, and sparks had left tiny burn marks on his leather apron.

Shelves above the crates of wood pulp and jute held rows of stemmed glasses, thick-footed goblets, flutes so slender you could almost see the champagne bubble, but also vases and bowls.

As the glass spun, the sphere faded from bronze to transparent. But the man with the web of veins on his face and the large, round eyes was not satisfied; he blew again, and the sphere grew into a thin-walled bubble, a balloon. I wanted to cry "Stop!" and "Ho!" worried that the sphere would explode into a universe, a cosmos with its own planets and laws. But then the glassblower pinched it with heavy, black iron tongs, as though it were not a sphere of glass but a lump of dough, and then there was a pair of spheres, one large and one small.

He ticked the object loose from the pipe, and when it had cooled off some, he filed the jagged bit where the pipe had been attached, as if smoothing out the rough edges of a theory.

The Geldersekade, like the Zeedijk, was crammed with taverns and brothels. Stuffy alehouses where boisterous, sweaty men sat cheek by jowl around a smoldering candle. Merchants, ruffians, jugglers, and acrobats for the fall fair; grain traders, pickpockets, seamen.

A matronly woman, a pinioned owl perched on her shoulder, told fortunes with tin pouring, cards, and palmistry. The wench's reputation was underscored by the low neckline of her blouse. With a pitcher of beer in one hand and five mugs in the other, she moved like a flagship through the putrid, overfull taproom. The customers looked from her to the tavern boy, a child at most, who pumped the bellows at the hearth.

An ace of hearts fell to the ground, a jug spun on its rounded bottom, someone got tugged by the hair, the blade of a knife glistened, two—three?—bodies rolled in a clew across the filthy floor. The owl let out a blood-chilling yelp and made a fruitless attempt to fly off.

The lawman, put out by being roused by the ruckus, cast a routine glance around the corner of the doorway, and before he could shut the door behind him, another senseless fight broke out, not worth his attention, and a dog shot past him, bone in its mouth.

When you grow up protected or privileged, as I did, you never lose your sense of security. You can roam where you will or even enlist on a ship to the East Indies, and you will always carry the stamp of the protected.

From a young age, I couldn't have been older than six, Father took me to the taverns of the Warmoesstraat and Buitenkant. He went there for business. The German tradesmen from Pommeren and Brandenburg and Danzig fell *wetterkrank* from the least puff of sea air and gravitated, with bloodshot eyes and dripping noses, to the nearest alehouse, grumbling about the noxious mist. They called for their liqueur of choice, "Danzigs Guldenwasser," Hanauer beer, and sausages, all the while bellyaching about how sick the Dutch weather made them. Father took advantage of their bleary-eyed malaise by cleverly negotiating lucrative deals with them.

"Blockheads," Father would say once back outside, kicking shut the heavy door to Inde Gulden Handt with his heel. "Nothing but blockheads."

I watched it all with the indifference of a blank-eyed fish, which must have aggrieved Father no end. I could not muster any real, let alone passionate, interest in the timber trade. My thoughts, my foundation, were with Mother and the spinet.

I had my fish look.

ALL I WANTED to do was sing. Like another person has feet that want to run or dance, like another has hands that want to forge or build, I wanted to sing, with my breath, my voice, my lips, in fact, with my entire body. It did not matter about what, I simply had to sing, without stopping.

My teacher at the Latin school, who taught us the quadrivium, and in passing gave us a dose of Hebrew and Arabic, was of the opinion that in order to sing, one had to get out into the world. First thirty years of study, then thirty years of travel, then thirty years of writing. He had learned this from his teacher in Ghent, who had learned it from his teacher in Lisbon, he in turn from his teacher in Toledo, who had translated Aristotle from Arabic to Hebrew and then to Latin, because that is what his teacher had advised, and so on and so forth back to Ibn Battuta.

"In your case, I'm not sure about the thirty years of study and another thirty of writing," Ben Yohai said. He had a face like the bark of an old holm oak. He spoke in a high, psalmodic voice. Sometimes he wore a beret, sometimes a kippah, then a bonnet and, on rare occasions, a turban. He was tall and slender. Black curls fell about his shoulders. His green eyes looked keenly around him, while his gait was as mindful and measured as a flamingo's, very much unlike Damascius with his jaunty, skipping way of moving about the lesson room. He boasted that he had been tutored in the humanist approach of Hegius in Deventer, teacher of Erasmus, a name he never failed to mention. "But see the world you must, to free and find your voice."

So, after Latin school I did not seek a mentorship with an architect; by then Father was dead, and I did not turn to the timber trade. Instead, I roamed through the fields and along rivers, slept in squalid, sultry inns and under trees with a mossy rock as a pillow, having learned from Homer to make a bed of twigs and leaves.

And I sang.

I sang all day long.

I roamed, and I sang.

I could not stop.

My voice, my mouth, my lips could not stop.

So it was. My teacher was right, and his teacher in Ghent and his teacher in Lisbon and his teacher in Toledo, who had translated from Arabic into Hebrew and Latin, and all those other teachers and also Ibn Battuta and maybe in the end also a Hindustani storyteller known for his frame stories, or a Chinese functionary at the imperial court, master of the pen, the cittern, and the sword.

I had to roam the world to find my voice, but most of all I had to become one with my voice, with singing, completely surrender to it so it would not become second nature but *first* nature, my first and only nature, shutting out all the rest so as to be oblivious to any kind of distraction.

I recognized this obsession later with the shamans, but by then I was well and truly ensconced in my ice grave, and I traveled through lower and higher worlds, egged on by their song and drumbeat. And with Willem Barentsz, who was above all an experienced pilot. Petrus Plancius was probably also driven by the same obsession, but I never met him. I did see him once when I was hanging around the market women who sold cheese and eggs on the Dam—I was fond of the lilt of their Zaandam dialect. I watched his crookbacked figure hurry into the Hoogstraat and disappear behind an oncoming cart laden with beer kegs. He had a reputation in Amsterdam in those days, and it was as though he sucked a whirlwind of whispers and voices with him. Together with my sixteen companions, I would serve as a pawn in his crusade to prove there was an ice- and land-free polar sea. Now it's his turn to be a pawn in my story.

WHEN I BOARDED the ship, it was the first time in my life, with the exception, naturally, of the inland ferries. I was a prematurely old poet with a few prizes already under his belt—it would have been strange indeed never to have won a prize at a literary *rederijker* evening, a *haagspel*, or a *landjuweel*, those rural or urban festive rhetoric contests—and one who could just as readily don the mask of a poet worn down by the vicissitudes of life as that of the cantankerous old writer posing as seasoned and wise; and that mask, too, could be exchanged for a more truthful one, and even my rightful face, if it could still be found under the many masks, had frozen into a removable mask.

I NEVER DID like the sea. Rivers, yes. The sea was too vast for me, disproportionately so, too sovereign for me to regard it with anything but awe. And once I had left my childhood behind, I became incapable of awe.

Ah, that colossal expanse, undulating like a worrywart blankly stuck on a single thought and boring you with it interminably. The vacant look of a dull-witted Boeotian. Something stupidly mechanical that blindly obeys the pull of the moon. For me, the sea was herd mentality, entirely antithetical to poetry, to the intangible, to caprice, to madness.

Rivers, though, flowed unhindered through my verse—they meandered, gouged out bends, dried up here and flooded an old town center there, not raging but simply curious, having a peek in the storage cellars: casks of jenever, barrels of pickled fish, jute-wrapped copper plates, reams of paper; and then there were their branches, their deltas that dispersed into the sea or into another river with one last glance back, an eddy.

Rivers are in our blood, while the sea is a vengeful deity as generous as it is demanding.

But even for rivers I still reserved a certain dread. I once attempted an outing in a sloop, armed with only a boat hook. No sooner had I pushed off but the boat capsized. The current dragged me along; I banged against a rock, and the sloop floated past me before I could grab it. The boat hook bobbed after it.

I liked rivers—from the shore.

During my vagabond days, I was fond of sitting on grassy banks of gurgling brooklets, unable to ascertain their exact source, glistening, murmuring, unsure of themselves, gradually descending down a shallow slope to a stream bordered by yellow and purple flowers, where sand martins burrowed their nests in the man-made walls of sand. I preferred currents to waves.

On my way home from school, I would often take a detour through the fields of daisies, buttercups, and thistles. Amsterdam was so compact that you needn't go far to reach the outskirts. The ground there was soggy, but there were plenty of windmills to sluice excess water via a complex system of drainage canals to surface basins. In the winter, you could skate on these frozen polders and flooded fields. I tied irons under my shoes and scampered—cautiously; I was well aware of the water under the ice—toward the horizon with young, energetic strides. The horizon was made for skaters. And, of course, for caravels, barks, and galleons.

A river in the distance meant motion, activity, hope. I watched the ferry to Haarlem, its passengers gesticulating as though carrying on discussions or exchanging news that had blown in with a just-landed merchant. Or they had witnessed an execution on the Dam and were demonstrating how the severed head rolled through the sawdust, or how someone was drawn and quartered.

Of all the birds, the geese were my favorite. Their flight, their calls, their V-shaped formations invited you to reach for something.

In the distance you could see Amsterdam's houses and spires, but most of all the many pile drivers: tripods around which fifty men tugged on a pulley to drive trunks into the ground, the workmen's song cheerfully echoing in the background.

I spent minutes staring at the tens, no, hundreds of flies on a cow patty, all of them in frantic, blind hunger for a bite of manure, unbothered by the crush. Something must have startled them—the shadow of a falcon, a gust of wind in the grass, or perhaps I slid off my shoulder bag's strap too abruptly—and they flew off with a furious hum in a frenetic moment of darting and glistening. Ten seconds later they were back at it, jostling one another in a disgustingly fanatic squirm of legs, greasy bodies, wings, and the flash of an emerald-green scute.

Then, a meter from the object of the flies' desire, a worm wriggled out of the ground. Calmly stretching and contracting, purple red with a white bulge about three-quarters of the way along its naked body. While now I have difficulty recalling my father's face—I do see him in his thick fur coat, but his face has faded to a blurry oval—the image of that earthworm is still sharply etched in my memory, even the grains of sand that stuck to its undulating little body.

Not for a single moment did I think of picking up the worm. Not out of compassion, mind you—I was guilty of performing the usual experiments on snails and frogs—but because no less than a miracle was occurring before my eyes. The worm, emerging from the earth like a blossoming flower, a declaration, a revelation, or a falling star. But the worm itself was enough to constitute a miracle.

Even though I never did anything that was forbidden, those days in the fields outside the city, along the river, were secretly wondrous. Loafing and lazing were the joys of my boyhood, which made me aware of an essence and condition of existence. The meadows were yellow with buttercups, dandelions, broomrape, hawkbits. The poplars rustled their silvery leaves.

At home, the kitchen smelled of cinnamon, bay, and clove, sometimes also anise. Or of nutmeg, if Mother rasped the hard nuts to mix with apples into the sauerkraut.

The house is wooden, with a thatched roof. I play with stones and twigs. Father leads a horse by the reins over a sandy path. From the open window comes the smell of cooking, and I could say it was the smell of pancakes, but I'm guessing my memory is playing tricks on me. The insistent hammering of a woodpecker carries from the woods behind the house. Grandmother, wrapped in a shawl and with sharp, angry eyes, crouches on the ground, scratches the dirt with a forked stick, and grumbles that the house is cursed. She scratches a cross in the dry sand. But here, too, my memory could be hoodwinking me. Even before I started school, we lived in a three-story brick house in Amsterdam. There was a shiny glazed-tile floor, a kitchen in the basement; there was a staircase, and another, and outside there was a stoop. My clogs had made way for leather shoes. It was quiet in that house, even when Mother, her dress chastely buttoned to the neck, sat playing the spinet decorated with an arcadian landscape. In the cool hallway, a Chinese vase held a single white lily.

WITH MY FOREARMS resting on the railing, my gaze drifting over the gray-green expanse, I was struck by an awareness of the immensity of the sea, but also of the sky, of the journey before us, one that might well bring us to the court of the Emperor of China, and the courage of the crew who, although more or less forced by circumstances to muster in, has embarked on a bold, monthslong voyage on barely negotiable seas.

One sailor, Pieter Pietersz Vos, if I remember correctly, sat hunched over on deck. We were sailing past a coastline of jagged peaks and deep, ice-clogged inlets. For a few days we had sailed along an island that some of the men claimed was part of Greenland. We saw reindeer and found, to our surprise—for we were well above 75°N—a variety of flowers: low-hanging willows, yellow poppies, entire carpets of tiny, star-shaped purple florets, and white flowers we learned to call scurvy grass.

For some days there had been an ongoing dispute between the helmsmen of the two ships over which course to follow: more northerly or more easterly. And now Jan Cornelisz Rijp was sailing away from us, and we from him. His ship chose to sail down the east coast of the newly discovered land, while ours headed straight for Novaya Zemlya.

Pieter Pietersz Vos shivered under his felt cloak. His teeth chattered. Slicked with sweat, the veins in his neck were swollen, bulging the tattoo of an anchor with a ribbon swirling around it.

The ship bobbed on the calmly rippling waves. The sails hung limp. A large bird of prey flew along the larboard in search of food, its brown-speckled wings flapping slowly and noiselessly. Then, with short, snarling squawks, it soared out of sight.

When the deckhand looked up at me, I noticed a yellowish glaze in his eyes. He opened his mouth, and it stiffened into a perfect, silent "O."

We thought we saw swans in the distance. They turned out to be ice floes.

"The calm, that's the magnet. It neutralizes the winds . . . The magnet," the terrified sailor squeaked. "A giant magnet is going to drag us down. We have to sail to the south, follow the coast. We're too far north."

Later that same day, his primitive fear would run up against the sobering reality of an ice-bogged sea, Pliny's thick, viscous waters. But for me, that magnet was Novaya Zemlya. It sucked everything toward it, dragged down galleons, fish, birds in flight, islands, entire swaths of coast in a seething vortex, a maelstrom leading to absolute silence.

Magnetic north hastily shifted from Canada to Siberia. I think it's the drumbeats. The jacks-of-all-trades, as the overeager child called them to his father, when he had been given an egg that contained an egg, which also held an egg and so on and so forth.

No matter where I begin, I end up at Novaya Zemlya.

FARTHER AND FARTHER we went. That was the motto of our century, the one that began in 1492. Farther. Farther. Beyond the known, into the unknown. We had no use for the notion of *non plus ultra*. Farther to the east, farther to the west. Farther to the south and farther to Thule, to Saint Brendan's Sea, to magnetic north.

Explore. Discover the world. Tap new sources of wealth and knowledge. The medieval fixation on the salvation of the soul after death easily could be translated into an earthly variant. "Go farther." Past death, past the earthbound—that was simple for medieval man, who of course did not see himself as medieval but as a witness to, and implementer of, the Revelation, the Apocalypse, and the promise of Redemption. While just a few generations before us, people had gazed at omens—the appearance of a comet in the night sky—that prophesied the end of this world and, at the least provocation, were overcome by rapture, our time set its sights on the discovery of new worlds. "Go farther." Beyond the known, as the sixteenth-century inquisitive, enterprising man understood it, and also beyond the commandments and dictates. Trust your own conclusions.

And man went farther, farther, ever farther, until that, too, became a commandment, a dictate, and he began to long for a smaller world.

But we lived the springtime of that to-be-discovered world. *Our* world, mind you—for there were plenty of other worlds to be discovered, and this discovery, or realization, that seeped into the feeling of superiority, was part of that springtime. There were other worlds, other suns, other solar systems, other gods, other aesthetics, other I's in an I. That fragmentation, that chaos, that joy!—and a golden opportunity for future malevolent leaders to win over those mortals unable to keep up with progress, by promising the restoration of the simplicity the left-behinds thought was lost.

I have seen much. I can see far. For four times a hundred years, I have listened to geese fly overhead. In the spring and in early autumn. There were years, just before the warmth kicked in, that fewer geese flew over. The shaman who taught me to observe pointed out a headland with watchtowers, barbed wire, troops in gray kit. There were hardly any watchmen, because whoever wanted to escape just flew into the great void. The men in Stalin's gray rags survived on goose eggs, and sometimes they caught a live one.

A wordless whale bounded out of the sea.

"The river here tastes like berries," said the fox to the hen. "Go ahead, slake your thirst. I'll keep my mouth shut."

I wait in the snow like a mammoth's tusk nostalgic for its mammoth. I went past the cold villages.

There is much I have seen. There is much I can tell.

A RAVEN COLLECTS pebbles in its beak and hurls them into the air. The pebbles become stars, and the raven bobs and hops with pleasure: it worked, again!

I PLAYED WITH the egg for a long time after that, but I never saw Father again. His faraway trips to the tracts of forest in the north and the east rarely lasted more than two months, occasionally three, perhaps longer if he was detained by war or floods.

Mother would usually start getting uneasy a month and a half into his absence. She would get irritated by my clumsiness; I was all thumbs, and even that was a gross understatement. If there was something Mother herself couldn't manage, she was quick to lose her patience. How many times did the sudden slam of a door or the spinet lid interrupt my studying?

And then, one day Father would turn up—imposing, energetic, with the self-assurance of someone who had overcome a whole host of tribulations in distant parts. But this time, Father did not turn up, not after three months, not after six months, and not after nine months. Mother's anxious pique settled into a quiet resignation that harmonized remarkably well with her usual good nature.

A year passed. A fellow merchant returning from his territories told us that Father had been arrested in Moscovia, accused of being a spy. He had been caught in possession of a map of the region around Yaroslavl and thrown into the clink. It was said he died in his cell before his case came to trial.

Later, we heard that an English rival had peached on him. Later yet, word had it that he had escaped or was released and was in Siberia, earning a small fortune in the peltry trade. This was the version I wanted to believe—Father had surely fooled a warden with some sleight of hand. I pictured it in detail: Father making a hunk of bread disappear, the flummoxed warden finding it in his own coat pocket. Father doing this kind of thing, also with a plate and cup, for four days running. But on the fifth day, nothing. No bread. Father tells the man he's got to pay attention. No, still nothing. Father doesn't believe him. He'll feel for himself. He pats the warden's clothes, locates his keys, pats further, and, holding the bread that had been in his own coat pocket the whole time, exclaims, "Look!" The guard stares at it dumbly and realizes he's been had when the cell door slams with a satisfied clang and Father locks it from the outside.

I had my egg, which contained a smaller egg, and in that egg a slightly smaller egg, and inside it an even smaller one, until I could hold the smallest, pea-sized egg next to my ear and hear Father's footsteps crunching in the Russian snow deep in the taiga, or stomping from the cold on a wooden raft, or hurrying across a field, or dancing in a ballroom.

I heard it all. That tiniest egg contained his footsteps.

ON THE WARMOESSTRAAT, I walked past the shop with the maps, almanacs, pens, and travelogues. The bookshop owner waved, beckoned me inside, his mouth moving noiselessly along with the gesture. He was, for a moment, a fish. A carp or a bream, swimming around in his own world, his lips roundly pursed. I went inside and felt underwater. The diffuse light glided with slow, algal swells over the large and small octavos, the world maps, the compasses, and the dish of sweets, fruits, and candied nuts on the counter.

"There's new paper just in, from Basel. Want to try it?"

He always found a way to lure me inside. Pistachios, which I loved—and from Gaziantep at that. Paper just delivered from a mill north of Amsterdam. Freshly cut pens. Gallnut ink and, later, Chinese ink. I hesitated outside, at the grammars and dictionaries, and looked through the pale-green windowpanes at his gestures—a meaningless, banal image at the time, but accompanied by a presentiment of something that later, in retrospect, will have greater significance.

The fish began to speak.

The bread spoke.

The light broke through.

The chalice tipped over.

The bread multiplied and the new bread also multiplied into nearly same-sized portions, which in turn also spontaneously multiplied without losing any of their volume, and there came no end to all this multiplying.

The image of the bookseller in his shop, gesturing to me from behind the window, would often crop up in my thoughts. Like a secret message in coded language that promised to reveal the mystery of the world, but, before I had deciphered it, dissolved into that turquoise underwater world.

He gave me paper, and I took a pen from the Rhineland earthenware jar; next to it stood an inkpot, and I wrote in elegant chancery hand, cursive, with copious curls and ink strokes, alternating between thick and thin. The paper gave, enough to allow the pen to dance, but was sufficiently stiff to subtly push back against the complex, swirling patterns garnishing the capitals.

The bookseller peered over my shoulder, his cold, dry breath grazing my cheek. He regretted having only learned Gothic script and not the Italian style. "Never got the hang of it, not really." When I looked up, I saw a vein on his temple quiver like a baby eel.

I lifted the pen from the paper. His eyes were damp. I had written a few lines of Hendrik van Veldeke. A droplet of ink, a tiny black pearl, formed at the tip of the pen.

I was too young, too naive, perhaps still too much a part of Mother's closed world, to register the bookseller's excitement. I shared his passion for books, for stories, for the power of words, but also for craftsmanship, bookbinding, paper, and ink.

His hands were a landscape. From under a torn thumbnail grew, like from a crack in the pavement, thistles, plantago, dandelions. His knuckles were a mountain range that painters, tradesmen, and inquisitive astronomers crossed to reach Italy. The *amo-amas-amat* and *φιλω-φιλεις-φιλει* echoed through the cluttered workshop; the bookseller smeared panels of a chestnut-wood box with hide glue, folded linen or leather around a book cover, and corrected me if I incorrectly conjugated a verb.

The droplet on the pen grew.

"Beautiful," said the bookseller.

"Hendrik van Veldeke, but you knew that already."

"Your handwriting."

I switched the pen to my left hand. The bookseller moved to give me another quill, but I waved it off and wrote, from right to left in Arabic, the opening lines from a poem by Ibn Khafaja. I knew he couldn't read them, but he was as delighted as I was with the script's gracefulness, the way it resembled birds in flight.

A REMOTE COAST with sheer bluffs, inlets, and a small boat or two in a bay, a Russian single-sail lodja, and three houses or a cloister. A typical sight in this frigid desolation. Craggy coastlines, the screech of hundreds of thousands of gulls, petrels, razorbills, then a few more houses—hardly more than shacks—lean-tos, fishing huts, and, farther along behind a palisade, a cloister.

A coastal vessel drops anchor in the bay. Monks leave dried fish, reindeer skins, vats of fish-liver oil in front of the cloister gate. That same day, the wares are loaded onto the ships, out of which come bales of woolen cloth, kegs of beer, earthenware, iron tools. The boatsmen leave it all at the gate.

And then, out of the blue, a band of warriors dressed in thick coats and trousers, bow and arrow slung over the shoulders, comes whooshing, almost hovering, across the snow. They glide on sleds with ash-wood runners, they leave salmon and sealskins behind in exchange for what they take with them, but their exit is a blur, so swiftly and silently they've vanished into the distant white.

As the ship sails out of the bay, the monks bring what's left for them across the courtyard, through the refectory and into the storeroom.

THE PERMAFROST IS a sound box through which vibrations resonate over vast distances.

Seismic tremors, volcanic eruptions, tsunamis reach my icy grave with a menacing rumble and crunch; they shake me up and then move onward and gradually die out in the distance. The tectonic violence of the Lisbon earthquake was an experience of prophetic power. A vision of the world rent to pieces. The eruption of an Icelandic volcano is always welcome; the waves of warmth it brings every few decades are always full of voices and song, half a sentence, a telling metaphor, a recurring refrain.

But for now, it is still. It could be still, in all senses of the word, for years on end. Still and cold. The frozen ground is impervious to water and roots, but not to voices, sounds, whale song, acoustic vibrations of any sort. I could hear a seal scraping the surface of the ice to keep its diving hole open. If the ice was thin enough, I could hear him bang it open with his snout, followed by a playful bark and splosh.

Only very rarely did fishermen pass by. The Russian of these Pomeranians warmed me—figuratively, of course, but in the sense that the thought of it can have a physical effect, even if it's only in your imagination.

They lived on Russia's northern coast. They live there still. They hunt, they fish, they set traps, they skin seals, they skin polar bears, they skin Arctic foxes. They stretch hides on a rack, they chew the skins to soften them—perhaps they learned this from the Samoyeds, or it's a bit of knowledge that wafted over like pollen; they sew jackets, shoes, trousers with needles made of reindeer or whale bone. They know, without the aid of a map, the contours of the coastline, the capes and bays, the islands, the hazardous bluffs, the dead-end sea straits, the inlets where seals sun themselves on the rocks, the pools where fish mate. They trade with the Samoyed people, monks, Russians in Arkhangelsk, and sometimes with the crew of a passing Brabant ship.

The Pomeranians' Russian warmed me with its *zh's* and *tch's*, which, like miniature locomotives, *zhwished* and *tchugged* through the sentences, propelling the syllable-heavy words. Maybe if I'm making comparisons, I should evoke Arabian caravans that trek through the desert like a string of Russian words. But I've been lying here for four centuries. There is much I have seen. There is much I can tell.

There was also a sound that resembled my wooden toy egg, a sound that contained another sound, which in turn, like a teardrop of gold-colored glass in which a complete insect with all its legs was trapped, held a sound where the *zh* and the *tch* lay all helter-skelter, deciding at last to cut an unpronounceable deal that made you think more of a steaming, hissing samovar than a consonant.

IN THE SULTRY air above the horizon are castles, white fairy-tale castles, shimmering palaces, home to the Emperor of China. You can marry his daughter if you are able to solve her three riddles of cold and warmth, of ice and night.

Functionaries do everything in their power to dissuade suitors from undertaking such a proposal and the fatal contest that follows. They've already had to clean up so many severed heads. The whack of the axe, the crack of the vertebrae—just try to shake that from a soul so practiced in subtlety. Sweep up blood-drenched sawdust. And then organize those funerals, inform envoys, put up roadblocks. Is this why they became the highest civil servants of the imperial court?

Think about it, young man: no one has ever solved the riddles; a single wrong answer will cost you your head. No suitor has ever reached the third riddle. The second riddle, no more than five. Ah and ay and ah, they went down like ninepins on the very first one. And still we're putting the heads in the grave beside the body.

Tadgio, with his angelic smile. Alfonso and his long blond locks. Adalbart, so proud of his three a's, all for nothing. Patrick, who guessed the first riddle but licked the dust with the second. *Licked. The. Dust.* Think of Patrick, young man, imagine his face when he had guessed the first riddle, and then his expression when he failed on the second. Think not of the princess's beauty, think of Patrick and the extinguished gaze on his severed head. Think of Roemer, who fainted on his way to the scaffold. Or of Yuri the singer, or of Ibrahim, whose neck was so thick that the headsman needed three tries to chop it off, after which he himself was sentenced to death. Ferdinand, who stuttered and for whom the princess would have relaxed the rules if she could have done so without losing face. Pavel, spurred by his horoscope, read by a fortune teller in Prague who promised him great riches in China, alas for him. Tariq, with his bravura and his many colorful scarves. Vainglorious Francesco. Eyvind, so young; Claudio, a first-class braggart. The born comedian Alessandro. Job the brewer. And the mandarins, well-versed in the teachings of Confucius regarding good governance, road building, urban infrastructure, the division of goods, digging wells, and reading the stars, these indefatigable keepers of the imperial annals were the ones who had to gather up yet another head with bulging eyes.

In the sultry air above the horizon were castles, white fairy-tale castles, shimmering palaces, home to the Emperor of China and his daughter. All we had to do was sail to the horizon, continue east-northeast past Novaya Zemlya, and then turn sharply to the south.

WE SAILED TO the next bend and beyond that the hoped-for Cape Tabin? No. We sailed to the next bend and beyond it the corridor to China and Cathay? No. We sailed to the next bend and beyond it the Northeast Passage? No, only a few fishermen's huts. We sailed to the next bend and gave it a name—Kaap Oranje or Kaap Troost or Kaap Hoop or Kaap Plancius or Kaap Herinnering—and beyond it we could already smell the spices of the East? No, there were racks of hides and fish hanging out to dry. We sailed to the next bend and drank from teacups of translucent porcelain? No, there was floating ice. Icebergs came at us. Icebergs like the Last Judgment. Ice floes crunching over one another with a force that could wipe out a town or half a city. We sailed to the next bend and saw the veranda of a white wooden house? Yes, we saw a white wooden house with a veranda, in front of which passed a snow-white horse that shook its mane, and we saw ice, more ice, dissolving into mist, in white manes, white as ice, so that our eyes lost their way in all that white and all of us, sea legs or no, held tight to the railing, the rigging, the tackle, a hogshead of tar.

NOVAYA ZEMLYA IS everywhere.
Novaya Zemlya is everything.
Novaya Zemlya is my ruin.
Novaya Zemlya is my salvation.

ALL THOSE EYES in the cabin. Eyes that swam through the frozen hell but found nothing at all to latch on to, so they turned, defeated, back to their owner.

A long, dark night-day of hunger and boredom, of hanging in bunks, staring at the fire while Barentsz's caustic little beard gauged the mood like the needle of a compass, the magnetic pull of potential discontent and mutiny.

White flags hung in front of our mouths, but we did not surrender. Who or what would we surrender to? If only we could.

Mutiny? It's a catchy word, like keelhaul and grapnel. Two crew members were keelhauled during the previous expedition to the North. They had stolen hides from the Samoyeds. When it was discovered, they tried to save their own skin by bringing up one of Plancius's latest sermons, about the need to guide the heathens to God. They pointed out the planks dotting the landscape that the barbarians worshipped, a clear example of misguided superstition that needed to be quashed. But the captain did not fall for this red herring, this so-called mission to convert the savages. From one of these crewmen, only a torso and a few limbs reappeared on the other side, nothing else.

And besides, how *do* you keelhaul a man when the sea is frozen?

A week later, a couple of crew members hatched a plan to mutiny. They spat on the deck, looked knowingly askance at each other, grunted, nodded as a sign that the moment had come, and the next day they dangled from a gallows to the north of the Waygats Strait as illustrated in, yet again, the German edition, but not the Dutch, of de Veer's *True and perfect Description of three voyages, so strange and wonderfull that the like hath neuer been heard of before.*

Adventures?

Heroism?

Don't make me laugh.

It is one huge yawn. Nothing at all happens above the Arctic Circle, or at least it happens so slowly that our lives go by too quickly to notice.

Every activity here, no matter how banal, is by definition augmented by hardship and unimaginable cold. A face with ice. A pioneer's icicle-hung mug.

We know them.

Derring-do collides with a centuries-long yawn.

PETRUS PLANCIUS COLLECTED everything: journals, logbooks; sketches of coastlines, no matter how poorly drawn; portolan charts; tables with measurements of the depth of the sea and of the deviation of the compass needle, to the east or to the west, the phases of the sun, the trajectory of the planets; descriptions of harbors, sandbanks, capes, currents, ice drift.

Documents from incoming ships were sent to the Admiralty to confirm whether the sailing instructions had been followed correctly and that wages would be paid. Then Plancius was given leave to pore over the mountain of paper. Thorough and focused on the details, he examines the logs, the maps and drawings, his eye trained to spot the most minute scribble that could clear up a geographic dispute about magnetic north or an as-yet-undecided issue regarding the position of an island near the Moluccas, or open up new maritime routes; he is on the lookout for correlations, random events that can be incorporated into a *generaal groot werck*; he takes the steady stream of observations brought back by mariners and sifts, weighs, and purges them of inaccuracies, miswritings, and unmitigated nonsense—he knows who exaggerates and who fantasizes—and translates all that information, drawn from such disparate sources and of varying quality, into a map a pilot can sail by and which invites the helmsman to refine the abstract illustrations with his own observations, and so on and so forth, producing ever-updated and improved maps with every new expedition.

Around that same time, another scholar is just as fanatically—maybe even more so—collecting and exhaustively cataloging information. It is the Danish astronomer Tycho Brahe, who has repurposed the former hunting lodge Uraniborg on the island of Hven in the Sont into an observatory. He gazes at the heavens and observes phenomena, rhythms, planetary orbits of unmatched beauty, and in doing so triggers a shock to the conceit and vanity of cardinals, emperors, bishops, rulers of every ilk—those men who presume themselves not only sovereign but also divine.

Petrus Plancius sticks to sea currents and the problematic determination of longitude, the solution to which he thinks he has found in magnetic declination; he limits himself to the astrolabe and sailing instructions, and although he has added a few constellations to several celestial globes, these do not disrupt the status quo as violently as the findings of that gold-nosed mathematician on his island between Denmark and Sweden.

Plancius—or Plantius, as it is sometimes spelled, but also Platevoet or Platefoet—draws, accurately and in proportion, a map of landmasses, oceans, climates, coasts, bays, cities, towns, roads, harbors, rivers, bridges—of crucial importance!—mountain ranges, lakes, even volcanoes; he indicates forests with shading, illustrates cities with a walled cluster of houses and a church; he draws the beasts of the forest and in the sea, vessels, whales, dolphins; a compass rose; all of it situated in a net of horizontal and vertical lines, the "degrees" with which a navigator can set out a course. He colors in the map: light green for wooded areas, darker green for dense forests; oceans are deep blue, coastal waters light blue; he writes the names of cities in red ink, the smaller ones in black ink, mountains in brown and gray, and silver for the city where he sits illustrating this very map, where he lives among cartographers, engravers, booksellers, and which city—to its own surprise and by way of fortunate circumstances for itself and bad luck for the others—has emerged as the world's mercantile capital and will eventually be overtaken by other cities, once those places' stars align, until it is their turn to be surpassed by yet other cities that believe their good fortune and prosperity make them invincible.

STRETCHED OUT IN the grass under a powdered oak, propped up on one elbow, I held the toy egg in my free hand. The meadow, bisected by a cart track, sloped down toward the river; its long, lazy bends evanesced into the shimmering heat in the distance. The birds were still. A bumblebee buzzed from flower to flower. A whiff of honeysuckle wafted over from the woods, tickled my nose, and then, like a fickle beauty, slipped out of that short-lived dream.

I pulled the egg apart into its two halves and did the same with the smaller egg inside it, and with the one inside that, and the next and the next, until the smallest, unopenable egg lay in the palm of my hand. Unblemished and smooth, light brown with minuscule specks. I held it, as I often did, to my ear and heard the whacks of an axe. Quick, potent blows into fresh wood that echoed across the taiga. Beyond the Ural, through all of Tartary, until they reached Cathay and the steppes where stout-legged Mongol horses galloped.

The trees rustled in their falls and sighed as they hit the ground. All was quiet. Until the sound of an adze striking a recalcitrant trunk deep in the forest echoed like the one o'clock church bell on a sweltering summer afternoon.

Blow after blow. In blue-tinged woodlands, where timber rafts bobbed down the river, larch and silver fir trunks dried on the banks, slime mold grew on birches, and old women collected berries in a birch-bark pouch and sold honey in linden-bark pots at the crossroads, and where Baba Yaga, in a cloud of suppositions, stirred her steaming cauldron of tea steeped from violette roses on the right bank of the Ob, Pechora, or Yenisey.

That is where Father journeyed, where he made his fortune in the fur trade, while his slippers with the turned-up toes sat in the hall next to the Chinese vase, for years on end.

I roamed over fields and heather, through meadows and forests. I stretched out in the grass and chewed on a reed. And threw my shirt onto a willow, hung my trousers over the branch of an alder, tossed my stockings on a stone, and stepped into a lake.

I used to like to look at the River Waal where it approached Nijmegen from the north, curved westward, and carried on between its wide banks. In the still, low-hanging mist, fishermen set their traps, the ferry was loaded with carts and livestock, the passenger boat was still moored at Nijmegen. Cows on the riverbanks, willow brush, farther along the ever-mangy sheep rubbing against the scratching posts, crows at their business, the contours of the hills of Arnhem and Kleve. Rings appeared on the surface of the water where a fish nipped for air. A horse looked up from his water trough. Milky sap from a reed dripped down my chin.

With my knapsack draped over one shoulder, I would wander into the woods, following the smallest and windiest path I could find. The meadows, too, have their narrow paths, visible only from close-up, cleared by sheep or goats, by churchgoers heading home or lovers on their way to the woods. The sky was endless, and under the motionless clouds, carts were piled high with sacks of grain for the local gristmills.

The morning was with me, and I was with the morning. And with Father, with his riddle about the precious stone. He had his theatricality and I had my bravura. I was at the age where the resemblance to one's father becomes evident, and I surrendered to that sentiment without regret or revulsion, seeing as he'd been dead, or absent, for fifteen years, evaporated in the vast Russian expanse, and was not there to trouble my adolescence.

He wore his sable fur cloak with dignity and élan. I wore Mechlin lace cuffs. I flapped them as I shook loose my hands, cleared my throat, and, after a dramatic pause, sang, melodious and stately, beating time with my left hand, trusting my sonorous voice, not quite a bass, nearly as elastic as a tenor.

Father was a storyteller. I was good at declamation, maybe a bit too good. It was as though, after three or so poems, the words would take on a life of their own, so I would almost lose contact with them. My mouth recited the verses perfectly, but because it was so effortless, my mind wandered off to a game of chess or a new map of the world, and I found myself improvising, inventing new lines. I was two people at once, and it was impossible to tell who was the marionette and who held the strings.

I wrote in elegant cursive, my wrist cocked, caressing the paper or parchment with my pinkie, not for support but just for the pleasurable sensation. The chancery script, the flowing *litterae latinae*, exuded the new spirit of panache, cosmopolitanism, thirst for knowledge, drive for exploration. Pretty flourishes, the forward flow of the connected letters—a far cry from the chicken-scratch Gothic script.

From my first tentative foray into the rhetorical society De Egelantier—I was still a student at the Latin school—Roemer Visscher took me under his wing. He must have heard about my father's disappearance from his contacts in the grain trade and the cabotage around Arkhangelsk. While we were about the same age and were evenly matched, I knew it was up to me to realize his unfulfilled dreams. With his limited talent, he clung to rules, applying himself to our young, as-yet-kneadable language. But he raised his daughters with the objective of complete freedom. What a fine fellow he was! I leaned on him, learned self-confidence from him, and then left him behind.

After an evening of Chablis, lute, and song in one tavern or another, Roemer and I made a beeline through Amsterdam to the house of Hendrik Laurenz Spieghel, under the guise of being hungry for some new coinage, a clever pun, or a debate on a variant of a word, but mainly to dip shamelessly into his wine cellar.

"Off to the debate."

"One man's grammar."

"Three men's clamor."

"To whet our teeth."

"To wet our whistle."

"To gorge."

"By George!"

"To groan."

"Homegrown."

I gushed about Ronsard, whom I had hardly read. Roemer went on about rhetoric. I sang a moving song about a gazebo in a private garden, a basswood branch dripping with morning dew that scraped my cheek, droplets of blood forming a little row of vermilion pearls. Roemer scowled and lectured me: I had to mind my meter.

"Amice," I retorted, "I'll leave the hexameters to you; sing an iambic ode, if you must, in praise of a stadtholder or grammarian. Grant me the roses of life. May my song shatter the roof beams."

We were young, we were poets.

I'VE ALWAYS loved an impending snowstorm. The air becomes quiet and close, it takes on a gray shimmer that is profoundly humbling.

We still lived in the house with the thatched roof. A crow paced in restless circles around the stone edge of the well. Something was brewing. You felt it all day in the expectant, freezing air. Above the trees, the sky slid from gray to a warmer gray, a deeper gray, a saturated gray, a heavily pregnant gray. The sky could cast off its cloak at any moment. I was sent off to bed. I believe I saw the first flakes fall before I dropped off, but I could just as well have fabricated the memory.

The next morning, I awoke to utter silence, so deep and all-embracing that I lost my bearings. The snow was piled halfway up the window. The front door was partway open, and outside, Father was busy shoveling out a tunnel.

Grandmother was sitting at the hearth. The flames, made unruly by the draft, scattered shadows and flares of orange in turns across her face. The fresh wood crackled. She was usually up early for the chickens; after that, while I ate my breakfast, she would read to me or tell me a story about what had supposedly happened during the previous night.

"My eyes are tired, and who knows what's wrong with my tongue. Why don't you tell me a story?" she said with a faux-helpless chuckle. I often had the sense that Grandmother was concealing something, concocting some plan, but in a distant world where other rules applied. I was on my guard around her. But this time, even though I suspected some tomfoolery on her part, my reservations were quickly dispelled. What happened to me, I don't know, but the sudden role reversal, combined with my suppressed, silent euphoria about the nighttime snowfall, allowed me to be seized, nearly to the point of ecstasy, by my own words. I retold the stories Grandmother had read to me so many times. She listened, her eyes closed, a blush on her cheeks, her lower lip trembling at certain passages. Her unconditional attention spurred me on, lifted me to a level where the words just kept on coming. I was still a lad, had not yet started school, but I had discovered the power of memory and the gratification of playing with what lurked there. If I made a subtle change—an improvement for the sake of tension or the depiction of a character or the complications stemming from some incident—then Grandmother opened one eyelid halfway to give me an amused, probing glance.

Grandmother had seen something in me, something drowsing inside me that could be as easily shaken awake as lost for good, and she used our snowed-in shanty as the perfect place to bring it to life.

It sufficed to say, "There once was." "There once was a snowstorm." "There once was a grandmother." "There once was a raven." "There once was a preacher." "There once was a preacher who was also a cartographer." "There once was a city." "There once was an island." "There once was a bookseller." "There once was a river." "There once was a ship." "There once was a clock." And off you went, adding details along the way. "There once was an island, and its ground was always frozen." "There once was an oaken ship with pinewood masts from Riga." "There once was a city, and its harbor silted up." "There once was a bookseller who kept a dish of sweets on the counter." "There once was a bookseller who wished he'd learned chancery script." "There once was a bookseller who was always sharpening pens." You expand the scene to two characters if you want dialogue, three if you want intrigues. "There once was a bookseller and a boy." "There once was a grandmother and her grandson." "Go on," Grandmother said, her eyes still closed. The fire swelled, and Grandmother's face tingled from the heat and the thrill. In my memory, it's a single image, unclear whether Grandmother's face glowed because of the fire, or if her radiance made the fire surge. Transported by words she knew inside out, that she had read to me from the book of her memory and that I could now reproduce down to the last detail, she surrendered completely to the unfolding of the plot as though hearing it for the first time and as though the fate of the characters was being determined then and there, next to the fire after an unprecedented nighttime snowfall. "There once was a grandmother and a boy who learned to say 'There once was' from his grandmother." Father shoveled a path through the snow. "Go on," Grandmother said. "And don't stop."

WALRUSES CRAMMED THE shore at the mouth of the fjord. Hundreds of walruses, packed together as though they were a single creature, side by side and half on top of one another, an arbitrary patchwork of tails, heads, skin folds, tusks. A ripple that started somewhere on a single glossy coat traveled across the multitude with subtle throbs and quivers and the occasional quiet groan. Even when the ship's shadow partly fell across the mass of bodies, it did not faze them. They did not budge. Nor did their eyes, if you could even make them out among the folds of skin, show any sign of curiosity. We did not exist for these unwieldy creatures. Their lethargy was a world of its own, a lethargy that was transformed into stunning suppleness the moment they entered the water, grace coupled with strength. The light gave their coat a cool, silvery gloss. One walrus heaved a sigh that undulated across the huddle, returning once it reached the last walrus and meeting the first, weakened ripple in slow-motion interference. If one of them shifted, you could suppose—a stretch of the imagination—it had an itch. The insects teeming around a cow patty that I gaped at as a child was something you could understand, but this was different, something entirely new, so utterly unlike anything else that you could only sink to your knees in amazement or respect, setting aside the conceit of your own powers of reason, the classifying, ordering, assigning to known categories. At that moment I felt something I had not thought I was capable of feeling: awe. The walruses pressed up against one another, and what I saw was a mass with its own dynamics. The only thing that came close—the spirit always looks for something to latch on to, does it not—was the jellied fruit on a porcelain dish in the kitchen in the basement of the new house in Amsterdam.

WE SAILED THROUGH unknown waters, and Jacob Sterrenburgh shouted from the crow's nest, "Land!" and it was ice. He shouted "Ice!" and it was a polar bear. He shouted "Swans!" and it was ice.

We wound up at Novaya Zemlya. It was—obviously, although because of the mythologizing of the whole affair, one might forget this point—not our goal. China was our goal. Cathay was our goal. To round Cape Tabin, pass through the Strait of Anián, and then head southward to the fragrant and colorful markets of Asia—that was our goal. Pepper, nutmeg, silk, porcelain. Open up a new trade route. A northerly one.

Had it succeeded, that is to say, if Siberia wasn't Siberia—such an expanse fell outside the scope of our understanding; even the most renowned geographers and cartographers of the day had no inkling of it—if we had succeeded in passing through the cold northern waters to Japan, China, and India, then we would have slipped into oblivion. Sure, we would have been given a hero's welcome in Amsterdam, with fireworks, salvos, and cannon blasts; the blare of trumpets; cheers and hurrahs and festive hubbub on the Dam; we would have been decorated with ribbons, and for the ceremony we would have observed decorum and removed our white fox-fur hats. The mayor would have given a speech praising Amsterdam's courage, enterprising spirit, and determination, and afterward we would have been invited to sit at the banquet table. I would have written my ode and recited it at the festivities—a piece of garbage, but in the euphoria of a new gateway to unheard-of riches, it would have been lauded as a verse of Homeric proportions.

Who still knows Houtman nowadays? *De* Houtman, to be precise. Cornelis de Houtman? Ring any bells? While we were stuck on Novaya Zemlya that winter, he rounded the Cape of Good Hope and sailed on to the East Indies, breaking the monopoly of the Spanish and the Portuguese. But no one talks of this expedition, or of this captain who meant more, far more, indescribably more, for trade and for the later VOC than we did; all we did was give ridiculous, unpronounceable, to the Russians, names to a few capes and curves in the coastline of a couple of remote Arctic islands.

You can be heroic in utter failure, while success often looks easy. Pat, a bit dull; nice for the salon crowd back home, but rarely able to withstand the judgment of later generations. Triumphs and success stories sound alike in the end, but every fiasco and debacle is unique. But you knew that already, thanks to that Russian, what's his name, Turgenev, Dostoyevsky, no . . . Pushkin? No, not him either . . . Two syllables. Gogol . . . Yes, Gogol.

WE ENTERED INTO the deliberate darkness of the polar night, that derisive shadow waiting for you like the open maw of a predator. It only has to open its mouth and wait until bedraggled bunglers like us walk into its blackness. Munch, swallow, and gone.

We were caught in the trap the North had set for us, the trap that had already surprised, and would continue to surprise, so many travelers, explorers, and huntsmen, but also musk ox, caribou, and reindeer: the trap of the sudden cold, which like a dull, serrated knife twists it way through your bones.

For three days, the ice held the ship securely in its grasp.

For four days, five days, the ice held the ship in its grasp.

Six days, seven days.

For eight days, the ice held the ship in its grasp.

A WALRUS OBSERVED us from outside the high-water mark, looking anything but well-disposed at the vessel and the activities of the creatures on its deck.

A polar bear took in the scene without giving it much thought. He would satisfy his curiosity later. He knew we were sailing straight into the ice's trap.

An Arctic fox, his senses piqued by a mélange of unfamiliar smells, stuck his nose into the air, flared his nostrils, and gauged sweat, fatigue, tar, rope, and iron, which, suddenly reminding him of the liver of a polar bear, made him hawk up a hair ball.

A goose flying overhead noticed, amid the white of the snow-covered land and the white of the ice floes, the pale white of ineffectual sails and quickened its wingbeat.

A bowhead whale heard with its sensitive skin and even more sensitive double blowhole a banging, scraping, and prying, signals unknown to him that spoke of a distant struggle being waged.

HERE I LIE in the eternal ice at the north end of Novaya Zemlya, spontaneously freeze-dried when I was committed to the earth four centuries plus a few decades ago, with the understanding that the earth was snow and the snow would soon become ice and that it was January and that it was 76°N at a place where, unlike Spitsbergen, already known to us, there was no warm Gulf Stream and we were in the midst of the Little Ice Age. All my cells, thanks to the sudden and, postmortem, almost immediate exposure to the intense cold—luckily they kept the psalms and the Bible readings short—have retained their vitality. No life force has been sacrificed. My death was a mirage. A hallucination. The hibernation of a polar bear.

I have seen much, of which I will tell.

The mania of the intellectuals and the merchants. Open up a new sea route. Give your name to capes and bays, to seas, islands, and countries. Countries! Outwit the Portuguese and Spaniards, put one over on the English. The riches of the Orient in just a month. Oh, the eagerness. But it was slow going: rigging out a flotilla. Negotiating, negotiating, constant negotiating when yet another city threw a monkey wrench into things, when Middelburg or Enkhuizen proposed a different route. Naming skippers. Soliciting crewmen, a ship's barber-surgeon, an interpreter. Stocking up on provisions: sacks of barley flour, barrels of beer, vats of wine, pickled herring, casks of salt pork, beans, peas, dried fish, hardtack biscuits, Jisp zwieback, cheese, oil. And then the merchandise, my God, the merchandise that went on board. Goods to trade en route and gifts for the Emperor of China. Prints with religious and Biblical themes, earthenware, bales of velvet, pewter goods, plaquettes, washing jugs.

All for nothing.

All that courage. The euphoria, the lucre, the craving for fame or scientific recognition. And all that big talk and self-confidence. The ships equipped for adventure, for the discovery of the passage and the reward of 25,000 florins.

Nothing.

Shipwreck.

Ice drifts.

Death.

Gangrene.

There they sat, the seamen, in their stale, stiff rags, huddled together in a clammy shelter. Sunken cheeks, blank stares. Bodies accustomed to activity, to climbing ropes, scrubbing decks, lugging tar barrels, chests, and bales; the skin on their palms split from the rigging ropes, from hoisting sails and reefing them down. It stank of men, sweat, pelts, dried leather. The oil lamps burned bear fat, from which the occasional air bubble escaped with a gurgling hiss. The crew gazed bleary-eyed from their wooden bunks built against the wall. Jacob Jansz Hooghwout murmured prayers to Saint Pancras—to cure chilblains, it was said. The carpenter . . . no, forget the carpenter . . . the carpenter was dead.

Getting out of your bunk was a real event. Small things became big things. Big things, however, did not become small; they simply disappeared. We ate, we slept, we ate porridge made of barley meal and melted snow; we drank beer that tasted of resin; we checked the traps. The days, which were nights, flowed seamlessly into one another. We flipped the hourglass, we ate porridge of rusk crumbs and melted snow, we slept, we dragged firewood, we spooned the idea of porridge from our wooden porringers, we flipped the hourglass. Each day become the other.

Hunger nestles in your eyes, it presses against the back of your eyeballs, it is a hollow pressure, a nothingness that takes control of you with an oppressive, sickening emptiness and the knowledge that this emptiness won't soon be filled. It is a black hole into which everything vanishes without ever having existed.

But, in fact, we were more sick than hungry. Bleeding, shriveled gums. Scurvy. Words I had not earmarked for my ode. Teeth loosened and, one day, fell out of your mouth or wound up stuck in a hunk of fox meat, like fate's dice, a deposit on Charon's fare.

Laurens Willemsz slipped and fell while cleaning the fox traps. He lay there quietly for a few seconds, but in those immeasurably low temperatures, a few seconds equaled a fatal half hour. Remaining still meant certain death. Was he resigned to his fate? Could he not muster the energy to get up? Perhaps he could, but what about another day, ten days, a month? Two months of biting on your bleeding gums day in, day out, summoning up the last of your strength to drag driftwood, and then after that last bit of strength, summoning up some more?

He then began to thrash about. His head whipping in short, furious spasms. Up, down, up, down. It was a horrifying sight. As though you're granted a glance into the abyss of insanity, its superior sovereignty knocking you off-kilter. He chomped at the snow. Wheezing, panting, grunting, he attacked it until he no longer had the strength to move his jaws.

He lifted his head and gave me an astonished look, like a clown whose makeup has run. Snow stuck to his mouth, nose, and forehead, in his hair; it glistened on his eyelashes and his eyebrows but melted on his lips, which had turned crimson. It was as though I could feel their warmth radiating from that mad, convulsed face.

We all had moments when we would have gladly thrown ourselves into the snowdrifts, ranted into the wind, or blindly, recklessly charged toward a polar bear, jumped from one ice floe to the next, into the void, the distance, beyond exhaustion, beyond the night, in a liberating rage whose price—death—was more than worth it.

We saw our blindness, our darkness, the self-concealment. As soon as we saw our blindness, it took center stage and was no longer blindness. Behind that concealment we suspected a deeper concealment. This succession of coming to light and darkness upon darkness had no end, trapping us in a *regressus ad infinitum*. All knowing creates not knowing. That was the polar night.

LIKE THE ARCTIC fox, I could rely on my fur, regally white in the snow, dirty brown when the tundra thawed. It was the gentle atmosphere in which I had grown up. Mother at the spinet, Father in his fur cloak, that treasure trove of gifts and magic tricks. In those years, life's hard knocks became milder, they lost their edge. I couldn't, nor wished to, waste my sensitivity and intellect on failure and disappointment. So around that fur grew an aura of cool aloofness. It shielded me from pressure, and also—I say this without regret—from love and companionship.

It could have been otherwise. Once I joined a group of migrants fleeing the south. I hoped, by blending into the masses, to safely cross the restive border region of Brabant and, via Dordrecht, reach Leiden. Sunken, dusty, unsmiling faces that seldom spoke; scared children with furrowed brows. They were bent, weighed down by their belongings tied in blankets. Some of them had hastily piled their possessions onto a cart.

In addition to the scourge of bandits, there were the vagrant infantrymen who had either deserted or formed their own militias, led by a self-appointed captain. They offered their services to the highest noble bidder and were as fickle as the wind; if no count or duke or city hired them, then they claimed their own fame, plundering, raping, and pillaging as they went.

The refugees had escaped via a secret gate of a city under siege, wading across inundated fields. Or else they had fled as a precaution, fearful of the fury of the Spanish mutineers or the disordered *geuzen*, the lawless Protestant rebels.

At a crossroads in the woods, a heavily laden cart came at us from the east, followed, presumably, by a stream of displaced people. Pulling the cart was a tired donkey, whose head hung low and swayed to and fro with every step. Only a cart and donkey. No line of followers, no one sitting atop or amid the piled-up household goods. An ambush? Where the woods opened up onto a small clearing, the donkey stopped, with no intention of taking even one more step. A woodpecker hammered away; a red kite circled above.

Sheep bleated in the distance. A shepherd called out "*Louw, louw*" to them. A dog barked.

Then the furniture suddenly started shifting. A round-faced girl with eyes like saucers leaped down and did a cartwheel. She was followed by a tall, thin man wearing a three-cornered hat and bells on his ankles. And with some more thudding and clunking, down tumbled a chest, a cardboard crown, a drum, two wigs, and, at last, a fat man whose mouth was pursed into a blushing pucker.

Chairs, benches, and stools were set up in a semicircle in the clearing; there were cushions and pillows with blue tassels. Cords with colored pendants strung between the cart and the trees were enough to suggest a tent.

The tall man sat on the donkey, now undone of its yoke, and began drawling out a song. The girl pulled a shawm from her red velvet jacket and joined in the ballad—one of those this-and-that numbers, I love you and you're so far away, man and woman, childhood woes, and now we've grown old. The fat fellow trumpeted with his lips and slapped a march beat on his belly while the girl—a young woman, upon a closer look—wove into it a melancholy melody on her flute. She had an elastic face that contorted into a happy mother, a witch, a sulky child, a haughty duchess. The singer was a sullen harlequin, but when he grinned you felt for your purse to see if it was still there.

Decorative panels went up. Mountains appeared. The beanpole, draped in a lion's skin and wielding a cudgel, strode comically, heron-like, after the woman, who disappeared into a cave. The fat man hovered above the scene like a thundercloud, casting an immense shadow. This was meant to frighten the audience, and it worked: children clung to their mothers, a few boys bolted straight up in their seats, mouths open. And for this one moment, the bodies floating in the Schelde and the taste of dogmeat were forgotten.

The fat man flew—he actually flew—but with difficulty, flapping and puffing, and if he fell, he would crush the girl.

The donkey brayed, the panel flipped to the next scene. The backdrop was as blue as a lake, and the man who had just been flying stuck his grinning mug above the surface of the water. The two other actors each sat high in a tree, twenty meters apart. The girl, a dandelion clenched in her teeth, tossed a blue ball to the thin man. And then a red one and a yellow one—three balls going back and forth, and then a fourth, a fifth, until you couldn't count them and it was just a wondrous streamer of colors.

The water mirrored the sky, no trace of the man, ah, there's a bubble, some gurgling, a few more air bubbles, they burst, then one more bubble which burst too.

The donkey shouted, "Applause! Applause!"

The woman, with her round face and big, hypnotizing eyes, had an open, unspoiled look precariously balanced between mischievous and timid. But in her agility, her boyish jerkiness, was also a masculine firmness of purpose.

I felt the momentary, liberating urge to join this troupe of actors. Because of her, because of the brash bounce of it all, because of the abrupt changes of scenery, the youthfulness, the energy. For me, its antics and pranks were *terra incognita*.

The impulse subsided as quickly as it had welled up. I didn't need to become someone else. I remembered the words of my teacher, Samuel Ben Yohai; now, after years of schooling and years of travel, it was time to shackle myself to the writing table.

Turning my back on the clown-like and elusive face of the young woman—at least, by not tagging along with them for a season—marked the end of my nomadic years. My diligence and discipline of the next few years were equally proportional to the regret for that missed chance, but to be honest, it was beyond my capabilities anyway. I was more architect than acrobat.

The ribbon and pennants were rolled up; the cushions, chairs, and benches returned to their disorderly heap on the cart. The donkey, without command, walked to its yoke and let himself be harnessed while he munched one last strand of grass.

The refugees, depleted and destitute, resumed their silent trudge. Their rags smelled of exhaustion, smoke, and broken lives. Their frozen expressions offered no details but left no doubts. As they passed, a goat being led by a rope nonchalantly left a trail of droppings like ripe berries. A woman with a headscarf, wrapped in many layers of clothing, held down the lid of a woven basket, from which a mocha-brown chicken had just stuck out its head.

I walked via Dordrecht and Leiden, where Plantijn had just opened a bookshop, to Amsterdam. I had been wandering for the better part of a decade. By the time I toyed with the idea of joining Willem Barentsz on an expedition to the North—it all started with a chance comment by Roemer Visscher in De Egelantier: merchants were putting out their feelers for a poet who dared to take part in a bold venture—I realized, to my surprise, that another ten years had passed. This coincidence did not acquit me of free will, but the symmetry—the architect in me!—broke my resistance to the idea of spending weeks or months belowdecks with a smelly band of uncivilized jack-tars.

I, darling of Fate, would entrust myself to the sea. To the water, the element I feared to my core. I thought of Samuel Ben Yohai, his lessons, his advice, how he penned the letter aleph like an angel toppling backward, his remarkable green eyes like lamps but also black holes, the poems by HaNagid and Solomon ibn Gabirol. It was as though I could hear him say I had to go wandering again, only this time over less familiar roads.

Although for me the sea remained a soul-destroying phenomenon—I was probably using that harsh judgment as a way to ward off the fear—in one respect I was not disappointed.

Time and again I was struck by a blissful feeling of dizzying emptiness when the ship rose up on the crest of a wave and did not smack back down, but rather kept floating, almost weightless, on the next wave, as though lifted into the air by a pair of invisible hands.

I experienced this wave of visionary vertigo as poetry, the brief moment of levitation during which the first line of a poem comes into view. An indeterminate state where boundaries vanish, or where you're sitting atop that very line.

ONE EVENING, WHILE I was leaning against the mast, looking at the stars, barely visible in the white night, and thinking of good old, safe Amsterdam—the Oude Brug, the joineries, the bookshops, the rhetorical society, the house where I'd gone to live following Mother's death shortly after my years of wandering, the house with the stairs, the tile floors, and the basement kitchen, the women market vendors on the Dam, the thrashing fish as they were dumped from barrels into buckets, the hunchback Petrus Plancius—in that night when twilight merged into dawn, as though there was no night at all, which in fact there wasn't, and the iridescent clouds lit up the sky and the sails hung loose, I suddenly saw Father: not as a memory, but truly there, on the deck in his fur coat, his energetic face full of adventure, fresh out of a wintry forest.

He closed his fist, and when he opened it, knuckle by knuckle, finger by finger, water dribbled over his palm and through his fingers and dripped gently onto the deck. He shut his hand again, opened it quickly, and flames shot every which way, like scurrying salamanders. It was a new trick he'd learned from a

Finnish enchanter. He talked excitedly of Karelian birchwood. He had slept on a raft in the middle of a lake, was sung to sleep and awakened by the melancholic, ghostly call of the red-throated loon.

"But those insects," he said, "ruin everything. Ravens might have created the world and humankind, but after a while boredom set in and it was decided to give man an extra challenge, or to taunt him, so they created bugs. If I'm asleep on a wooden raft, can you swipe a mosquito off my nose with an axe without waking me?"

Father jumped overboard and vanished as the waves closed over him. Then Samuel Ben Yohai came walking toward me. The sea had become a sandy path, and the horizon was the edge of a forest. He walked with a slow, cautious gait, theatrically jabbing his walking stick into the air before arching its tip to the ground. The ship's deck had also turned into a path. But I could still hear the tap of the walking stick. My teacher stopped where the two paths crossed, his arms stiffly at his sides, his eyes shut as if listening for something. He smiled, nodded, opened his eyes, and extended his hand. "Here it is. Here. You've found it. Look." He walked over to the boulder marking the crossroads and scraped his wrist against it. Blood dripped from the wound, minuscule droplets like grains of sand. Master Ben Yohai dabbed his finger in it and began to draw on the boulder. Human figures, animals, signs of the zodiac, Hebrew letters, alchemic symbols. "This is it. You've found it. The Stone of the Dnieper." And with those words he evaporated into the white night.

THE WIND HERE is tangible.

In the Arctic, the wind is not a rustling tree, a flapping sail, a rattling roof tile, a piece of paper fluttering over the ground, something that might whip around a corner.

Here, the wind has the magnitude of the sea or the night.

The wind is something to be survived.

But it is also as tangible as a friend who demands the most from you. A friend who is used to getting his way and never faces pushback.

The wind can do what it likes here. Acknowledge that, and you're a step farther. You realize how fruitless it is to be an obstacle. You have to internalize that freedom and play the game.

I've had more than four centuries to ponder this and other matters. A human life is too short to reach more than one insight. And even that—having an idea, a real idea—is the privilege of only a few. Before you even begin to understand your fears and desires, death is looking you in the eye. Who will benefit from your life experiences?

The wind is a good teacher.

WE SAW MIST.

We saw fountains.

We saw a whale. I should just leave it at that. A sixth or seventh crewman, however, claimed to see not just a forest or just a monk, but a monk in a forest, writing. He said he could read what the monk was writing in his large book, and because imagination within the imagination has an evocativeness of its own, I choose not to omit the testimony of this sixth or seventh deckhand.

He, the monk in the forest on the back of the whale, wrote about a book that he once, long ago, before he traveled to the North but lived in a monastery, had burned in a fit of anger, because he, the monk, was a bit of a hothead who could not tolerate being made to read fables, nonsense, utter bunkum—from costly calfskin parchment, no less. In that book, bound in pigskin, he had read about three heavens and that when it was daytime on his island, it was nighttime somewhere else, that kind of piffle. It didn't even mention a forest on the back of a whale. Boiling with fury, he hurled the book into the fire.

Once he cooled off, the monk decided to travel through the only genuine and true world in order to dispel these ridiculous notions once and for all. That's how it is with temperamental types: one minute they're sitting quietly with a book, the next minute they explode in anger, and the moment after that they pack their bags.

And this monk, whom the monk on the back of the whale was writing about, came upon an island. He went ashore, gathered bits of wood to build a small fire to dry his shoes, and the island rose until it became a hill, and that hill turned out to be the smooth back of a whale. It started to rain, not a gentle sprinkle but a forceful spray coming from the blowhole, which the whale hoped would cool off its hot back. The wind caused the drops of water to fan out, which not only doused the campfire but sprouted seeds—plants that covered the surface and trees that shot up toward the sky. The monk was reminded of the book he had burned, and his cheeks had hardly begun to flush when he decided to write a new book in which he would undo that earlier misdeed, because in the only true and genuine world there was indeed a place for a forest on the back of a whale, and he would write an account of it. The story of an irascible monk, like the one he once was, who, upon reading unmitigated rubbish in a book, does not hesitate to throw it into the fire in his cell. To the blazes with it! But the next moment he joins a ship's crew so he can see all that nonsense for himself and unmask it as the Devil's chatter. Ah, ah . . . it ends with him, ashamed and remorseful, in a forest on the back of a whale, writing a new book about a peevish monk who—and on it goes, endlessly, if we're to believe what that one seaman said he saw after days of mist, white on white, gray on gray, haunted by bugaboos and egged on by the fantasies of his crewmates. But he wasn't far off the mark, because from books come more books.

A WILLOW IN the polar tundra that germinated when I was interred in my ice grave has now—after four hundred years, more than four hundred years, after four hundred years, a couple of decades, and a few years more—a trunk no thicker than my thumb. An extreme concentration of vitality that reduces mammals to bit players in a slow, stubbornly tireless world.

The trunks that washed up on the shore of IJshaven, worn down to bare roundwood by ice, sea currents, and rushing rivers, are exotics from a lush foreign forest. In fact, we seafarers, explorers, Northeast Passage–goers had more in common with those pines and larches ripped from Siberian woodlands than with that dwarflike willow that measures its life not in years or decades, but in centuries.

Our cabin was once, in these parts, the eighth wonder of the world. After our departure, however, the Ural storms and tundra typhoons did their work in an onslaught of perpetual hostility. Furious winds bashed against the front door. Nails were given some play, saw their chance, and sprang loose. The roof caved in at the chimney under a two-meter-deep layer of snow. Beams hung crookedly in a strangely hinged trapezoidal formation until, after pulling and twisting and warping in one weather depression after the other gale-force wind, they collapsed into the tangle of a Gordian knot.

A polar bear spent four days tugging at the loosened but still tightly wedged door until he gave up, frustrated. By the time he returned a week or two later, after inspecting the cracked and abandoned ship, he could walk inside unhindered, aside from having to stoop to get in, and in the end, his curiosity was more satisfied than his hunger. He licked the taste of fish, without being able to tell what kind, from the copper kettle overturned next to the hearth. He batted the kettle around the hut just for fun, ate a calfskin shoe, shredded the Amsterdam flag, and, finally, hurled the firedogs into the corner where the mostly caved-in roof was still the closest to its original height. The ruins did not budge; they did not joggle or jar.

I camped out in my thick layer of frost, gradually regained control of my senses, and learned, after a few lessons from a shaman who breezed by, to put them to use. When I sent my sight out on reconnaissance, I saw the polar bear sniffing an inkpot. The place only barely recognizable as our winter quarters was in such a state of confusion that I couldn't tell if it was my inkpot or Gerrit de Veer's, Willem Barentsz's, or Jacob van Heemskerck's.

Candlesticks, tankards, pans, the brass skimmer, a leather money pouch, drumsticks, and lead weights lay willy-nilly about the place, and strewn among spoons, pewter salt holders, halberds, a shirt with one sleeve raised as though waving for help, a wooden flute, the bronze bell; all this among a pile of dishes, plates, and oil lamps. Mendoza's book about China peeked out from under a skein of wick yarn. The whetstone had rolled onto its side, shoes were strewn everywhere, as was a jumble of keys, nails, coins, even the tiny polar bear carved out of a bullet, the sounding lead with traces of tallow and grit in its hollow core, the wooden bowls from which we ate our porridge, groats, colorless beans, the 1596 Deventer almanac, knives with bone hilts, muskets, files, chisels, the trumpet, packs of prints by now all stuck together, the ivory delousing comb—Pieter Cornelisz's pride and joy—pliers, rapiers, tar brushes, a compass, and, of course, the chiming clock meant for the Emperor of China that would never tick or chime for him.

From this array of furnishings, clothing, earthenware, tools, and weapons, the polar bear chose to sniff an inkpot. I retreated into my frozen zone with this image as a souvenir of our expedition: a polar bear with its nose in a small, square, lead container—one I might have dipped my pen into, or else Willem Barentsz or Gerrit de Veer—taking in the smell of ink. What images might that aroma have aroused in the bear? What does the smell of dried ink make a polar bear think of? Something tasty? Danger? The enticing unknown of an animal being roasted in the distance? The dank air of a winter den, the pungent odor of his mother's fur as she nursed him?

I had reconciled myself to this being the finale to our expedition to the Northeast Passage. A polar bear and an inkpot. Over and out. Basta. Kaput.

WE WERE STRANDED on Novaya Zemlya. Trapped in ice and the polar night. It marked the end of our mission and the beginning of our fame. We did not collect the 25,000 florins but achieved a dubious immortality. We were stuck not in just one polar winter, but one lasting centuries, in second-rate, overblown, nationalistic poetry and on the name plaques of public schools. *Vanitas vanitatum.*

All the fuss started in the nineteenth century. Give me the ink-blotched eighteenth instead. Let everyone try out his pen. Should that result in Schiller or Goethe, fine, as long as the masses keep their cool and don't get carried away with nativist doctrine. Nothing gets anywhere without ink blotches. So give me the eighteenth century, with its painted wallpaper, idyllic landscapes, bloomed grapes, shepherdesses, and then, as a foil to all that: *"Liberté, Égalité, Fraternité."*

Here I lie in eternally frozen ground. But eternity is no longer eternity. My top layer is getting restless. Things start to stir in the June spring, and by summer, or an attempt at summer, it's my zone's turn.

The nineteenth century needed heroes. You can call a nation into being, it happens everywhere, but what's a nation without icons? Without heroism, without an exceptional show of valor, the steadfastness and tenacity exclusively belonging to a citizen of this or that nation? Undaunted warriors fighting for the inalienable rights of this united folk?

For centuries, I contented myself with that image of a polar bear with an inkpot in its paw, heading across the ice and disappearing into a horizon of white on white, when a fur or seal or whale hunter, one Elling Carlsen, stumbled upon the ruins of the Behouden Huys on one of his poaching forays. Carlsen knew his polar classics, so he loaded the ewers, pots and pans, candlesticks, and oil lamps onto his sloop, the *Solid*, and as soon as he reached Hammerfest, he offered, via the Norwegian consul in The Hague, the whole lot to the Netherlands. No response.

No response?

No. No one in the Netherlands gave a hoot about the legacy of Willem Barentsz & Co.

I cherished my polar bear and his inkpot.

Carlsen eventually managed to sell it to an English tourist, who himself was then stuck with the lot because the British Museum wouldn't spare a penny for it either—wouldn't even take it for free. No conservator in Liverpool showed any interest. Southampton kept mum. Portsmouth looked the other way. No one anywhere in the whole Empire would buy so much as a pan or an oil lamp.

Then, only then, a year later, after a number of indignant articles in the papers, did the government of the Netherlands present itself as a buyer. And the hullabaloo, now that a sum of money was actually paid for it! There was no stopping it. Overcompensating for the original apathy, every nail, buckle, and hilt was greeted with exaggerated enthusiasm as if it were some seismic archaeological discovery. And this legacy—a history lesson grabbled together at a flea market and transformed into a national epos of intrepidness—was foisted on the Netherlanders, who hadn't even gone looking for the ice-cold artifacts themselves.

Our story lay there for the taking in the permafrost of Novaya Zemlya. It was ready-made, including sober heroism without eccentric bluster, in that time of nation forming, the days of yahoos, pioneers, explorers, and men of firm purpose who could look dry-eyed beyond the horizon. Our expedition was a flop, exactly what you get when you roll together pigheadedness, absurdly speculative theories, a blatant denial of the polar landscape, and an unwillingness to learn from native people who had lived there for centuries. It did not even occur to us to consult the Samoyeds as to clothing suitable for these extreme conditions—we were already savoring the scent of the orange trees of China.

If you're out for a bargain, a quick profit, a back route to Cathay, then you've no business in the North. You have to tailor your plans, goals, and intentions to the deliberate pace of −23°C.

Time is in abundance here. Time is gold at 76°N. Haste—carelessness—means certain death.

The monotonous, monochromatic, homogeneous landscape demands your full attention. Every detail must be allowed to sink in and combine with other impressions, to draw on an arsenal of experiences, saved as stories, to gauge one's chances:

chances in the hunt, chances of sailing through a just-frozen bay, chances of anything at all.

What did we know? We were trapped in the ice, in the freezing polar night, but even more unnerving, we were trapped in a story meant for somewhere else. With not any of the animals we killed—not with the puffins, gulls, brent geese, not with the Arctic foxes, not even with the polar bears—did we drip fresh water in their mouth as a sign of conciliation and gratitude. We saw only enemies.

We were a mistake, but that winter in the Behouden Huys took on epic proportions that we never again were able to shake off.

THERE ONCE WAS. There once was a snowstorm. There once was a grandmother. There once was a ship. There once was an island that consisted of two islands. You could also say "In that time" or "In those days." "In that time of wormwood and fire" or "In those days of snow and ice drifts." In the days that a bomb hung in the sky above Novaya Zemlya, a bomb the size of a whale on a parachute as big as a city. In the days that a bomb approached Cape Dry Nose—oh, if only Grandmother were here to read me the next chapter of the story.

In her time. In those early days.

Or you say "One day." "One day, a colossus too large for even the biggest Tupolev was slid into a bomber's cargo bay." "One day, a scholar discovered that you could use a bomb to set off a bigger bomb, which would detonate an even bigger bomb, whose heat would be of fearsome proportions, et cetera."

But how do you get a zeppelin-sized projectile into the belly of a flying whale? One day, the shadow of a bomb-within-a-bomb-within-a-bomb hung over Novaya Zemlya. If Grandmother had stood beside me now, she would have described the parachute, every bit of the 800 kilos of nylon, gram by gram, the scholars' excitement as they sat at the theatrically placed monitors in the military base, the steely and victorious expression of the pilot who was well on his way to becoming a hero.

In those days, when a polar bear encountered cracks in her usual route across the ice, when an Arctic fox pricked up its ears upon hearing a steady mechanical drone in a fatal crescendo, when a raven in vain scoured its memory for clues about this roar, and whales deep in the oceans sent out distress calls worldwide.

In those days, there floated above Novaya Zemlya a bomb unprecedented in the history of mankind. Well, what other history is there? As though there are bombs in the history of islands or the history of the snowy owl; yes, there are snares and chains, zoos and captivity and clipped wings, but bombs, no.

In those days.

IN THE ETERNAL ice, a solidified droplet of resin, and in it a fly, and in the fly a dream of a summer's day, the smell of reindeer blood, the concentrated sweetness of honey squeezed out of wood and the memory of the day when a teardrop from the fir tree washed over him.

IN THOSE EARLY days, when you could easily spend an entire week's budget on a book, a month's if you had it bound in Morocco leather with gold embossed letters and a metal lock, the world swirled through Amsterdam. In grain and wood; in musk, porphyry, sugar, and salt; in diamonds, emeralds, sapphires, and amethysts; in cloves, which, as everyone knows, warm the stomach; in beer, sandalwood, and coral, and also Afghan crystal and soap from Tripoli; in linen, silk, velvet, perfumes, aloe; in Arabic gum, licorice root, and salmiac. Who all peopled the Dam? Bankers from Augsburg, Armenian damask merchants, money changers wherever you turned, porters hoarsely shouting a path across the square, bumping into an Italian architect here, a Bohemian art dealer there, elbowing anyone in their way; market vendors from Westfalen, hawking pots from Cologne; farm women from Assendelft, plying a meager trade in cheese and butter; a French stonecutter, asking the way to "La Roccin"; drifters, their legs wrapped in filthy rags, addressing you in an incomprehensible dialect. A small crowd had gathered around a quacksalver hawking a wondrous elixir, his table piled high with potions, powders wrapped in cones made of pages from an almanac, ointments in pigs' bladders, pliers with which to pull teeth; amid all this, a cutpurse managed to make off with four money pouches, the contents of which he later, in a smoky tavern on the nearby Zeedijk, split with the quack. The innkeeper, who owed the lawman a favor—a trifle concerning closing times—saw this and grabbed his chance: the thief and his confederate spent that very night in the lockup in the basement of city hall. The jail's barred windows looked onto the square at ground level and let in the sound of metal chains scraping over the cobblestones. A skittish monk diagonally crossed the Dam, passing a surgeon heading out for a cupping cure, while a street preacher announced the end of the world. News was exchanged about deputations, appointments, exotic animals in Brazil, people in the Americas with their heads in their chests, giant turtles. Turbans passed by, berets, felt or velvet hats; beards straight from the Old Testament, soldierly whiskers with upturned ends, the meticulously kempt mustache of a connoisseur—a spy, perhaps—a Pole with a drooping soup strainer. Silk rustled, if you could hear it amid the shouting, the cursing, and the barking of the vendors. Children darted past, startled mothers looked over their shoulder. The smell of waffles made your mouth water, but this pleasure was soon countered by the nauseating stench of fish and the putrid odor coming from the canals. Chalk dust blew over from the stone market on the Rokin. The merchants, envoys, travelers, pickpockets, alchemists, migrant laborers, outcasts, seamen, adventurers, religious fanatics, and agitators—they came, they did business, they secured lodgings, they brought letters of credence, they stole, they opened a shop, they mustered on a cog to the Baltic Sea. They came, they left, they returned, they left again, but some stayed, including our very own Joost van den Vondel, the "swan from Cologne," whose grandfather was a linen weaver in Antwerp.

And then a Gerritsz marries a Jessurun and a d'Oliveira marries a Schoonhoven and a De Wit weds a Müller, and the granddaughter of Cremer and Mystliwska marries the traveling salesman Blondin, and one of their great-grandchildren emigrates to Canada and marries a Miller, and their grandchildren consider themselves full-blooded Canadians, but in the nineteenth century the great-great-grandchildren of Gerritsz and Jessurun swell with pride at the sound of the word "Netherlands," and one of them gets the idea to install plaques on Novaya Zemlya and Spitsbergen in homage to the heroism exhibited by Dutch sailors in the sixteenth and seventeenth centuries.

Illusions. Illusions.

They work.

They brought me to Novaya Zemlya. I stayed for four centuries, two decades, and a few years.

Illusions.

From stories come more stories.

An egg in an egg.

SOMEONE IN BRUSSELS, Leuven, Antwerp, or Ghent, let's say Leuven, the university town, has a theory about the circumference of the Earth and the makeup of the Arctic Sea. After a brief imprisonment, this theory flees along with its maker to the small and unpresuming city of Duisburg, a town really, a speck like so many other ones, therefore providing the carrier of that theory the safety of inconspicuousness and anonymity. He, Master Gheert Schellekens, alias Gerard Kremer, alias Gerardus Mercator, in the peace and quiet of his home not far from the market square, works his idea into a map that will inspire Petrus Plancius to his own speculative theories about the Arctic Sea, the ice conditions and open water in the North.

Plancius, too, aside from being a geographer, is a fanatical field preacher and therefore must also flee the Spaniards or the religious conflict or the civil war, depending on how you look at it, and he winds up, via Middelburg, in Amsterdam. There, his ideas must compete with other ideas for attention, influence, and capital. Other men—with money rather than ideas—have also fled Brussels, Ghent, Antwerp, and Bruges, seeking refuge in the Northern Provinces. They do not necessarily embrace Plancius's idea, but he still has, so to speak, the wind in his sails.

This translates to a small flotilla of ships full of men with ideas, skippers with ideas, pilots with ideas, trade clerks with ideas that vaguely reflect the original idea—and then the idea formed by this illustrious cabinet of thinkers is confronted with ice-cold reality.

If only I could start anew. Flick some lever the other way. Change a compass point. Have an ice floe drift in another direction. It would be asking too much for Antwerp not to fall into Spanish hands or for the harbor not to be blockaded by *watergeuzen*, sea rebels. But surely an apple could fall from a market stall and roll across the Dam, be stomped on by a wagoner, then by another, and then by an alderman hurrying to the assembly, and then, before any pinnace has set sail for the North, Petrus Plancius could slip on the apple, now mushed to a pulp, just at the moment that a mail coach pulled by four furious horses comes charging past, bang, boom, the cracking of a skull—surely that must be possible.

Is that asking too much of Fate? I see a mug with pointy ears, yellow eyes, and a potato nose grinning from ear to ear.

On a peninsula, two women toss an egg to each other. You can pull the egg apart, and inside that egg are two women who toss an egg back and forth. That egg, too, can be pulled apart, and you'll see two women tossing an egg to each other, and that egg comes apart into two halves, in each half a tiny woman, and they toss the pea-sized egg back and forth. They giggle like teenagers, and nobody gets the egg.

NEAR THE END of the northern glacier is a fjord where the people live in plenty. Children are born with seal fat in their mouth, and their mothers' milk is sweet with honey. Since the summers are short, the flowers grow quickly, and their bloom is so intense that their pollen and fragrance are ultraconcentrated. The whales swim to the inlet to drop their offspring, and seals sunbathe on the rocks.

A MAP WEAVES together facts and conjecture, coordinates measured with the most precise instruments and pure fantasy; it projects an ever-changing world onto a static, two-dimensional surface, subjects it to simplification, abstraction, and distortion, hypotheses represented in concise, symbolic language.

A map programs its user's viewpoint, and in that sense can prove itself to be "true." You see what the map tells you to see. You go in search of what the map lays out.

A map creates the reality it illustrates. If the map suggests a path where there is none, there is a good chance that, sooner or later, a path will be there.

The moment maps of the North appear, even with latitudes and meridians, the myth of the unattainable, barbarian, *ultima Thule* is broken. From maps come more maps.

A map depicts reality, and at the same time, by the choice of what it depicts, acts on it. A map brings about its own obsolescence.

What is not shown on a map is at least as significant as what is shown.

"He who travels according to a map," said the shaman, "sees the map. Throw it away. See the world."

He was right. But it's also true that maps awakened a curiosity in men, spurring many of them to see more of the world, to discover those parts not yet filled in. Atlantis, the Insulae Fortunatae, Pytheas's Thule—six days' sail north of the British Isles—the paradisiacal Vinland from the Saga of Erik the Red, Stillanda, Ixilandia, Estotiland, Drogeo. The allure of the blank areas on a map.

You can rivet your gaze on a map, and a map can open your eyes.

THE SHAMAN SANG until he was only voice.

He spun and spun until it lifted him off the ground, spiraling up to the world of the spirits.

The drumbeats were no longer separate strokes on a stretched animal skin; they had even stopped being rhythm. It was the churn of the Earth's axis, a whooshing between two worlds.

Such a spiritual journey was risky and demanded exertion. But more dangerous yet was the return from that boundless realm of the spirits, to one's own voice and footsteps in a world of resistance and boundaries.

During this hazardous transition, the medium could get stuck and find himself flailing on the ground as though in an epileptic fit, frothing at the mouth, sometimes with fatal results.

The shaman sang until he was only voice. He sent his senses —his sight, his hearing, his smell—across the tundra.

Then he whistled on a whalebone to call his senses back. With his eyes turned inward, he heard, he smelled, he saw, he felt what they had to tell him. Where a polar bear roamed, which ancestor's soul he had in safekeeping, whether they should kill it.

The enchanter reached for his spleen and knew where they had to wound the polar bear. The topcoat rustled, the bones, the raven's feet, the bear's teeth, and the dried feathers with their translucent shafts.

The drum is stretched with the skin of a sacred reindeer. On the drumhead, the cosmos is painted with the reindeer's blood. Above the line drawn over the drum's diameter, sticklike figures stand alongside reindeer and bears, which are drawn rounder, more voluminous. Under this line is another world where a figure in a flapping cloak floats about. He beats a drum on which the same cosmos is depicted, only smaller. Above the Earth with the stick-figure people, bears and reindeer are the sun, the moon, and the occasional star. There, too, a shaman floats; he's holding a drum, its head again depicting the cosmos, on which, among the moon, sun, and stars, another shaman is beating a drum on which the cosmos is drawn, with the identical layout of a center line, an underworld and an upper world with a flying shaman beating a drum, but you'll get a headache from squinting at the crumb-sized drawing on that miniature drumhead, so your imagination takes over.

The mystic wants to lure you into this circling, intertwining world. He will invite you to roam the world by asking questions. Where is Beringia? When must I switch from rotten fish to fresh fish to catch an Arctic fox? In which bay do the belugas mate? Such questions. And also: Who can forge the sword? What is as cold as ice but still burns? Or: What do I want? Who am I? What can I know? What can I hope for? What must I do? He will accompany you in the passage to a new phase in your life. He will do nothing; his presence is enough. His song and his drumbeats. He knows which mask you must put on: the Raven; the aloof Walrus; the Brent Goose, if loyalty is your path; the Snow Bunting, to whom you can always whisper your secrets and sorrows; the Arctic Fox, who will teach you to make do with scant resources; or the mask of the superior Polar Bear.

I sank into a grogginess that demanded no more effort than concentrating on the shaman's drumbeat. On the sound, the rhythm, or both, until they dissolved into the gratifying sensation of self-oblivion. The world opened up to me in countless guises that passed by, while at the same time I floated through them, without my skin grazing the surface of the animals or objects. I was in a trance. I breathed heavily, from deep down, from a calm world of endlessly long wavelengths and an amplitude spanning an eternity. My limbs flowed into a state of sublime lucidity. How long did it last, a second? Four hundred years? Was my entire journey to the North—the ravaged ship, the Behouden Huys, my death in the middle of the polar night—a séance evoked by a shaman? Time frames abound, and what was a second here was a century somewhere else. There was something next to me, a presence I couldn't see. Impossible to say whether it was outside of me or within me. The spirit of the shaman had taken over my body. I flew through the drumhead, to the other side of—yes, of what, actually? Where was I? I saw the Earth below me, not a few meters, not ten meters, but hundreds. If I looked up, I also saw the Earth. A raven flew toward me. It gestured for me to climb onto its neck. “Can you tell me stories? I have the key to the treasure, but must fly for days and days over forests. Nothing but forests. Endless forests. Tedious. Can you keep me awake with your stories? I always like ones about Artic foxes, how I can outsmart them if a polar bear has had its meal and has left a bit of seal lying on the ice. Or about Fenja and Menja grinding salt and the grindstone falling into the sea. Go ahead.”

“Do you know the story of the seafarers who tried to sail across the North Pole to China?”

“How about something more realistic? Otherwise, I’ll lose interest and still fall asleep. You have to make it plausible. Could be about me—about how I created the world.”

“But without the bugs.”

“Bugs?”

“Don’t tell me you don’t know about the bugs.”

“Well, to be honest . . .”

“There once was a preacher who was also a cartographer, and because in those days men sailed everywhere, across all the seas and to all corners of the world, they needed maps. But nothing was known about the sea in Never Warm. *Was* there even a sea? The cartographer who was also a preacher thought there was. He even thought there was no quicker route to the prosperous East than via Always Light.”

“Okay, okay, never mind the bugs. But men quickly forget that they must stay active. That’s why I gave them a tormentor.”

“To stimulate and energize him. Sounds familiar. Mosquitoes, bluebottles, those ones with the long legs. Get the picture? Bumblebees, crane flies, fruit flies . . .”

"Now you're exaggerating. I had nothing to do with fruit flies."

"Blackflies, then."

"Most effective."

"Let me continue. There's also an overwintering on Novaya Zemlya."

"I thought I'd been clear: make it plausible! Start with the snow geese, lemmings, or seals, a snowstorm—call it a blizzard if you like—aurora borealis, the trail of a reindeer, and you'll reach me soon enough. Begin now. There's the forest. And don't stop. Go on, and don't stop."

The drumbeats receded. The polar bear next to me was pregnant with two cubs. I couldn't see her, but her hide enveloped me from my dancing in place. The shaman had vanished, a tundra hare leaped off.

JUST BEFORE MY death, I saw a worm creep out of the ground, slowly stretching, contracting, stretching again, and with each peristaltic action changing color from violet to pink to purple. It was already half a meter long, and still it kept coming out of the ground, growing constantly. It wound its way up my leg, around my waist, chest, neck, mouth, and stopped in front of my eyes. The worm had no eyes but was looking at me. It was the watchman of the polar night. It spoke with a round, fishlike mouth, gave me riddles to solve and tasks to execute. I had to peel a stone, tie a knot in a soft-boiled egg without making a mess, split a hair with a dull knife. It quizzed me on the largest prime number, the quadrature of a circle, the exact time when all the heavenly bodies were put into motion, how many grains of sand fit into the universe, and how many Devils on the point of a needle. It asked where ideas came from, what the most valuable stone was, and fired off the next question before I could answer that one. Why the sea was salty, the number of heavens, and the number of torments of Judas on Sunday. And then I got a glass of jenever thrown in my face and was lowered into my ice grave.

I HAVE REMAINED here in the northeast of Novaya Zemlya, where derring-do runs up against hibernation and heroism dissolves in a whiteout.

I felt like an Arctic fox, first white, then gray, sometimes pale brown with a few black spots, then colorless; like a scruffy alchemist in a tattered tailcoat, the quack, the magician, the sorcerer, the miracle healer, the con man who sets up shop on market squares with his jars of salve, bottles of ointment, flasks of vague, syrupy elixirs, chirruping magic words and promises, in the hope of falling into favor with a ruler—yes, this is how those small foxes prick up their ears, listening for snow hares or too-slow sea coots, while they'd much rather just curl up against a polar bear.

I learned to travel through other worlds, where you can read thoughts and dreams, talk to animals, and win over spirits. Where there is no distinction between the physical and the immaterial. Where time does not pass. Where there is dancing, a whirling of air and waters and spirit and ideas. A spinning that is indistinguishable from standing still.

My body glowed with sweat. I shivered as in a fever, but I was in a trance, and my teeth chattered with ecstasy. My eyes turned in their sockets until only the whites were exposed.

I went through a snow tunnel.

I went through ashes.

I went through my mirror image.

I went through fire.

Dying is nothing. Easiest thing ever. But then comes the hard part. Then the petrifying starts, and you pull the power of the universe toward you.

I broke the Arctic silence that I have kept up for four centuries and which has hardened me.

I have made friendships here, not for life, but for death, for eternity.

A polar bear once kept me company for an entire winter. And then another winter. A third winter. A fourth. For five winters she dug her winter den alongside me. Six winters, seven winters, many winters in a row. She nursed two cubs in her half sleep. May my own hibernation, too, have been this fruitful.

I have seen much. There is much I can tell.

The layer above my ice grave became gradually more active, first in the summer, but then in the brief Arctic spring too. And now the active zone has reached me.

During these times of great change, when the question is whether this will be a turning point or at least a time of recalibration, I awaken from the ever-frozen ground.

Because forever is no longer forever.

This is my *cedelken*, my message, which I might not have tucked into a powder horn and left behind in the ice of Novaya Zemlya like Willem Barentsz did, but which is nonetheless my testimony to that overwintering.

Come, Great Thaw, come.

Come, warmth.

Come, let my words flow. For four hundred years, they have been lying here frozen.

Come.

AROUND THE TIME that more brent geese started flying overhead, by which I concluded that the prisoners' time in the trench mines was on the retreat, the construction of an icebreaker was nearing completion in a Finnish shipyard. Ah, Finland—by way of a cartouche, a diversion, a blank space to be filled in, an old-fashioned coda, a dissonant—where my father bought wood, haggled with saw masters, and slept on rafts. Finnmarchia, Finland, Suomi, Finlandia. *Yksi. Kaksi. Kolme.* One. Two. Three. Land of enchanters. Land of a spirited, sottish tongue that caprioles like a common tern. Land of the *kantele*, a cither made of the jaws of a giant garfish, strung with the hair of a stallion, with the gar teeth used as pegs.

The Finnish forests were not crisscrossed by rivers with the breadth and reach of those that flowed through the steppes and the Siberian taiga until they spewed drifting tree trunks into the Arctic Sea, which we used to build the cabin of our overwintering and our survival. The Finnish forests had less of the drama of raftsmen and risky currents, more of lyricism and lakes.

Father traded in Finnish wood. He told us of rafts the size of Texel in the lakes of Lappeenranta. He spoke admiringly of Finnish singers with magical instruments who could conjure and assume any guise: an adder, a June breeze, an eight on its side, a castle. No, those were no blockheads.

I regarded that as one of his tall tales, but now I know better. Now the great warming has arrived. Now I hear singing in the layers of ice. The landscape speaks to me. First, though, there were the booms, the deafening rumble and thunder.

It was your typical Finnish autumn that started in the middle of August, and by the next-to-last day of October 1961, rime and morning frost heralded the onset of winter. The Finnish were working tirelessly on an icebreaker, one of many as part of the country's war reparations to the Soviet Union. The hull was floated out that summer in a ceremony attended by Finnish President Kekkonen and the secretary-general of the Soviet Politburo, Nikita Khrushchev.

A bottle of Crimean champagne hung on its cord like a sacrificial animal. An Orthodox priest, at whom Khrushchev glowered as he loudly blessed the ship with "Gospode pomiluj" or something along the lines of compassion, mercy, and the Lord, loudly enough for tetchy Khrushchev to lose his cool. Just as he was about to storm off, the bottle swung and missed the hull, dangling unbroken back and forth. Nikita deigned to give the bishop a condescending smile, grabbed the rope, and flung the bottle at full speed against the hull, shouting, "Victory is ours!"

Meanwhile, work continued on the boat. On this thirtieth of October 1961, the windows were to be installed on the bridge.

Just as the glaziers were busy with the middle pane of hardened, extra-thick glass, designed for the extreme conditions on the frozen seas, as they attached the double suctions cups and were about to lift it into place, a colossal atmospheric wave came rolling at them and shattered the pane into a carpet of tiny glass splinters spread across the entire foredeck.

The workmen gaped at each other, while their arms, obeying the laws of inertia, momentarily hung motionless and empty-handed in the air. Seppo Karaaliinen was on the verge of chewing out his colleague Arto Kaukiumo. Arto Kaukiumo was about to lambast Seppo Karaaliinen. But before they could vent their surprise and ire with a stream of invectives at each other, a new gust came whipping over them, alongside them, past them, and made the newly installed panes shudder with a high-pitched tremolo. These did not shatter, but a tea glass dissolved in a sea of shards as though shedding its old self.

What blindsided the Finnish glaziers was no surprise to me anymore: nuclear tests above Novaya Zemlya.

IT WAS A clap of titanic force, a colossal wallop that, like in a thunderstorm, continued to roar and rumble, followed, terrifying in its suddenness, by a vacuum-like silence, not the kind of silence that offers relief or the space to exhale, not soothing silence, but a silence that dragged you into the abyss in a maelstrom of insanely intensifying pressure.

After the nuclear test, the drone of radioactive whispers went on for weeks, months, sometimes more than a year, a crackling sound like breakstone or hoar-frosted moss, an aggregate of the countless voices that had configured themselves into a sinister crepitation. Maybe the Oracle of Delphi spoke with this kind of rattle. To interpret it you had to be a priest of some order that did not yet exist.

The crackling subsided, settling into a murmur in which you could at times make out crystal clear, recognizable sounds. I heard a fisherman sing while mending his nets. Gulls screeched overhead, water sloshed between his boat and the quay. A woman took a wicker basket, put two rabbits in it, covered it with a cotton cloth, and went off to market. I heard the short, sharp, slightly muffled ticking of two sets of antlers, and when it went quiet, I knew that one of the reindeer had backed off, and at any moment the other could let out a triumphant bell. But sometimes the antlers stayed tangled, and I could hear the wrenching and chafing as the poor animals twisted themselves ever tighter into a fatal, knotted union in which they would starve, first one and then the other. I heard the roar of cannons, followed by the tinkling of champagne glasses once a ceasefire had been called or peace treaty signed. I heard pleas, entreaties, cheers, weeping, dry sobs, the crescendo of pleasure, cries from the deepest depths to the greatest heights. I heard men gambling under a sycamore, the clatter of the dice in the leather cup. The slurp from teacups, the sugar cubes dissolving, sucking on a hunk of rock candy. A bird skipping along a dry roof gutter.

The great warming was preceded by a radioactive drone, a whisper of voices, an underground current of sound waves.

The wallop that surprised the glaziers and shattered windowpanes in Finland was "Big Ivan."

Or AN602: its first official name.

Or RDS-220: as it was also called, never mind the dispute between the people who call it AN602 and those who insist it's RDS-220.

Or "Vanya": the name used by the Soviet authorities.

Or "Kuzka's Mother": a mistranslation of what Khrushchev actually said to Nixon.

Or "Joe 111": what the CIA called the test.

Or "Tsar Bomba": another of the West's nicknames for Big Ivan.

Big Ivan is the name the creators of the hydrogen bomb gave it. The device, many times more powerful than all the Second World War's bombs combined, was the brainchild of Andrei Sakharov. His lifelong fascination with the power of the atom resulted in this sensational nuclear test that proved more useful as a tool of intimidation worldwide than having any military, let alone scientific, value.

The thermonuclear bomb measured eight by two meters. I repeat: eight meters by two meters. Can you picture it, eight by two meters, big enough to spend the winter in? This hydrogen bomb is loaded into a Tu-95 on October 30, 1961. The Tupolev aircraft is painted with white reflective paint to minimize heat damage from the explosion.

The bomb's descent is slowed down by an 800-kilogram parachute, giving the pilot time to fly the Tu-95 safely away from Big Ivan before it detonates.

There, the bomb with many names hovers ten kilometers above Novaya Zemlya, just north of the Matochkin Strait that separates its upper and lower islands.

Big Ivan was designed as a three-stage bomb—a bomb in a bomb in a bomb. The first stage, a fission trigger, sets off two thermonuclear charges, which in turn bring about the powerful radiation implosion of the third and main bomb.

Big Ivan dangles from its parachute and approaches Cape Dry Nose. By now the Tu-95 and a Tu-16 observer aircraft with a camera crew on board are forty kilometers away.

The hydrogen bomb has now dropped from an altitude of ten kilometers to about four kilometers.

At 11:32 in the morning Moscow time, the explosion takes place above Novaya Zemlya.

The radioactive element uranium 238 has been replaced with lead, minimizing harmful fallout, but the shock wave is no less ferocious. The seismic wave circles the Earth three times. During its second pass, a tea glass shatters on the deck of an icebreaker being built at a Finnish shipyard.

That is what I know.

WHAT WAS ETERNAL is no longer eternal.
What was eternal is now voice.
What was eternally quiet is now flow.
Eternal is no longer eternal.
Eternal is gone forever.

No more is eternal.
Eternal is no more.
Forever no more.
No more.

Eternity of white dissolves.
What was for sure is no longer so.

Gone gone.
Gone forever.
Gone.

WITH ANDREI SAKHAROV I've brought together what I had to bring together, in a—no, wait, I know more, the hen said to the fox, said Grandmother. I know something. Ten years after Seppo Karaaliinen and Arto Kaukiumo had installed the windowpanes, another ship—the nuclear-powered icebreaker *Arktika*—smashes, with brute force and much differently than Petrus Plancius had imagined it, a path to the North Pole. Arto Kaukiumo would, shortly after this incontestable proof of the imminent triumph of Communism, die of complications during an appendectomy. His colleague Seppo Karaaliinen continues to the bitter end and to everyone's annoyance—including that of a great-grandchild, for Seppo lived to the age of ninety-three—to boast about the *Arktika*, which he "had built in the prime of his life."

The great-grandchild, whose name I never could fully make out here in my ice grave, works in international commerce and operates a great number of tankers and container ships. This involves vast sums of money. This descendant of Seppo Karaaliinen will soon decide that it is more profitable to set up her own bank, so that she can use other people's money to provide herself with interest-free loans. She also applies that idea to the extremely expensive insurance of the ships and their cargo, as well as to the ships' brokerage. Shortly after her thirtieth birthday, she will, once she has monopolized freight transport to China via the "silk rails," preside over a consortium of companies that pass lucrative contracts among one another, and she will name this holding, in honor of her great-grandfather, Arktika.

I can see this far.

I know something else, said the hen, said Grandmother, said the crow who walked in circles atop the stone edge of the well. The man who liberated the power of the atom—when mankind shrank back from the freedoms once cheered by Giordano Bruno and put him, the man who freed the atom, and others like him, into ragged gray uniforms and behind barbed wire—later, this scientist, who had survived his underfed and underwarmed infant years wrapped in his parents' musical scores, and as a child had copied the frolicking figures he saw on the delft blue tiles in his grandmother's kitchen, wanted, after the atomic tests, to also liberate the power of man, and he paid for it with exile, because whoever challenges the power of man must first travel through the mouth of the whale to its deepest, darkest belly. You go in reluctantly and come out—missing a leg, maybe—purified.

Now I really have brought together what I had to bring together in, as I said before, a less-than-coherent narrative, but my spirit, thawed out after four hundred years on ice, is like the drum of a shaman on which various worlds are drawn, and in those worlds there are drawings of a drum just like it, each with various worlds drawn on them, in which another drum with three worlds, and so on. It's enough to drive a person crazy. My memory has evolved in layers, which sedimentary subsidence made bleed into one another. The stories, the connections, the branching off—they mirror one another endlessly. And then Tycho Brahe and Johannes Kepler suddenly crop up. It could also be Petrus Plancius and Arminius. Or Copernicus and Bruno.

All right then, let's have Tycho Brahe meet Johannes Kepler, and Johannes Kepler meet Tycho Brahe.

It is 1600.

Or thereabouts.

It is Prague.

Or thereabouts. It could also be a castle or a fort outside of Prague.

Rows of candelabra holding serenely burning wax candles. Napkins of Flemish linen. Wineglasses of Bohemian crystal. Lackeys in mothy livery, standing sharp as switchblades behind the chairs. In the middle of the table, on a silver platter, a boar's head stuffed with mushrooms, berries, and hazelnuts. Some joker has put an orange in its mouth.

The emperor, the alchemists, the other thinkers; the rabbi, who is antsy because soon, on the orders of a sovereign he despises, he will have to revive his golem; the hand that sneaks three small tarts into a coat pocket; the court poet, whom no one listens to; the sparkling of silver and crystal; the whispering in the long corridors of the palace—they are an alibi, pure decor, a frame for the meeting, catalysts for two elements that must consummate their chemical union.

Alas, alas, I must interrupt myself again—let us scrap the entire decor of the assembled company and table decoration. No banquet. No bacchanale. The fortress is a farmstead. A single flickering candle sheds restless light. A sturdy lass sets two pewter mugs of beer onto a free corner of the table with reproachful thuds. *Plonk. Plonk.* The two men are focused entirely on each other and the papers spread out before them. They do not notice that an unruly lock of hair has escaped from under her kerchief, nor do they see how she tucks it back in as she walks off.

The man that measured and measured and measured—every star, every detail, the stars in relation to one another, the position of celestial bodies, paths of the planets, conjunctions and deviations—and then measured it all again, on his island Hven in the Sont. For twenty years he has been gazing skyward from his observatory and has drawn up tables, mathematical series, categories; the numbers, the figures, the position of the stars, the declinations, he lines them all up; refractions, measurements, cross-checks, *anomalitas coeli*, meteors, the Great Comet of 1577. They flutter like powdery snow across the pages, and before he can draw conclusions, he's calculating again.

This man of measurements meets the man who explains them—we know him from the Novaya Zemlya effect, and he explains them in a way that means the Earth must relinquish its central position to the sun, exactly as Copernicus had quietly claimed not so long ago, and, eighteen centuries before him, Aristarchus of Samos, and, even earlier than that, some Chinese mathematician. Now that the crystalline harmony of a stationary Earth, with its nine concentric rings, has been smashed to smithereens, Bruno cheers "the bursting of the celestial vaults," because he senses the promise of freedom that awaits therein—freedom, freedom for all, but what he cannot foresee is that mankind will have to face the infinite incertitude of that freedom.

A number cruncher meets a visionary.

A fusspot meets a man of the grand gesture.

A meticulous scientist meets an equally conscientious theorist.

A man of details meets a man of the world.

A man who observes meets a man who tells.

All right. Enough.

It's over. What began with Petrus Plancius, with a supposition about an open Arctic Sea, with the fall of Antwerp or the fall of Granada—1492 was another somber year, when the last stronghold of the caliphate in Al-Andalus fell and the Catholic terror was ignited—prompting the grandparents of Samuel Ben Yohai to flee to Antwerp and his parents, thirty years later, to Ghent and then Dordrecht, and later yet to Amsterdam, where he became my teacher who urged me to roam the world just as he had learned from *his* teacher who had learned that from his teacher, and he from his teacher in Toledo and he from—but now the sources become unreliable . . . enough, enough . . . What began when Grandmother, after that night of the heavy snowfall, said "Tell!" with Mother at the spinet and Father in his fur coat, what began with an expedition to the North, a ship broken by the ice but perhaps run aground on a sandbank, it all may end now.

And it ends by beginning.

I CAN RETURN to the map, perhaps this time engraved on the jawbone of a whale or the antler of a reindeer, or painted with alder sap on birch bark, the map spread out on Petrus Plancius's worktable under a galleon suspended from a beam, the map that plotted our route with a dotted line. The east coast of Novaya Zemlya stops at the Behouden Huys, where we sixteen men shack up for the winter. The chimney is a barrel from the hold of the ship that, like me, remains anonymous.

Spitsbergen is not yet called Spitsbergen, nor Svalbard. Whales spout their fountains, unaware of what awaits them. It is not known how far Greenland stretches, or if there's another island next to Iceland.

The map is all about Novaya Zemlya, where the winds can blow unimpeded, where tree trunks from Siberia wash up on the shore, and where the warm Gulf Stream has long reversed course.

This landscape is humbling; it makes you accept that you are weaker, lesser, no match for unimaginable forces that show their might as much in their quiet, deliberate blankness as in their unrelenting violence.

Novaya Zemlya was my ruin.

Novaya Zemlya was my salvation.

Novaya Zemlya is the Nothing you must come to terms with. You do that by grasping that this Nothing is All, that All and Nothing are the same thing. This can take years, decades, the best part of your life. I had centuries.

After studying with Damascius at the Latin school, we were well seasoned in the concept of the All and the One. In the white of the snow, the white of the Arctic mist, the white of the ice, in this white, reflective world where no one point is distinguishable from another. If I recall Damascius's words correctly, your spirit can either agonize itself into a madness with no foothold, or else experience the liberating emptiness of the All, of the All-One and the One-All.

That's a lot of capitals, too many for this space where exclamation marks and uppercases don't hold up.

The pounding or sometimes silent footsteps of a polar bear greet the snow. The nervous, sniffing tread of an Arctic fox greets the snow. Snow greets the snow.

Snow patiently covers the patience of lichen and dwarf birches.

In an endless alternation of frost and brief, but gradually longer, thaw.

THE CAVE BEAR emerges from its lair. The mammoth, stiffly awakening, looks for his tusks. A dream escapes from the melting ice. Swans shed their feathers.

I think back wistfully on my centuries in the permafrost, when the days were nights and the nights were days. When a polar bear in her lair kept me company all winter. When shamans, with their songs and their drumbeats, transported me to other worlds. When geese in a V formation flew overhead in the spring and early fall. When I heard a soft rustling, and it was the sniffing of an Arctic fox following the scent of a snow hare across the frozen tundra.

I've reached my end. Farewell, polar night, goodbye, adieu. See you again? See you in the next ice age?

I end and I begin; I begin and I end.

My words stream forth.

The Great Thaw has begun.

Granny, Granny, this is what is written in the book of the man in the belly of the whale who writes by the light of whale oil on a sheet of whale parchment. Last night I dreamed of that book. Now I know what he finds when he finds the book about which he's writing in the belly of a whale.

This.

I get up out of the ice and scout out new paths.

Novaya Zemlya is everywhere. I can begin wherever I want. Novaya Zemlya is everything. I can end wherever I want, and begin all over again. Novaya Zemlya is my ruin. Novaya Zemlya is my salvation.

A SNOW HARE leaps out of my chest.

The snow hare is a soul. It leaps out of the deceased and hops about until it has found a new host body. This can take years. It is a finicky soul that does not move into just anybody.

The snow hare does not need to hide; he blends in with the snow and the white nights. Sometimes in a word. But you just have to say the word out loud and off he goes. This is the specter that words leave behind and which affects you more than the word itself. The snow hare can reside in Cape Tabin, in Yenisey, in a turban, in porcelain, in scurvy grass. These are not hosts, but rather refuges or masks that he can put on at will.

Now that I've broken out of my silent zone, I will roam about as a ghost and whisper stories, words—ivory, porcelain, Ural, millstone, passage, amber—in people's ear.

Go.

That most of all.

Go.

Go, and I will call it Novaya Zemlya. That is, Nova Zembla. That is, New Ground. That is, New Earth. That is, New Land. That is, New World. That is . . .

Go.

THE SNOW, WHICH sparkles in a swirling dance of radiance, everywhere blue, green, purple, sometimes yellow and red, but without losing the overall sense of whiteness.

About Sandorf Passage

SANDORF PASSAGE publishes work that creates a prismatic perspective on what it means to live in a globalized world. It is a home to writing inspired by both conflict zones and the dangers of complacency. All Sandorf Passage titles share in common how the biggest and most important ideas are best explored in the most personal and intimate of spaces.